SHELTER ISLAND

Also by Carla Neggers in Large Print:

The Cabin
The Harbor
Stonebrook Cottage

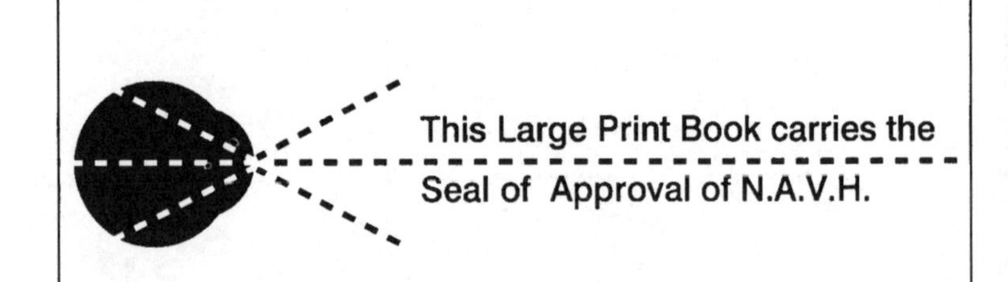

SHELTER ISLAND

Carla Neggers

Thorndike Press • Waterville, Maine

All characters in this book have no existence outside the imagination of the author and have no relation whatsoever to anyone bearing the same name or names. They are not even distantly inspired by any individual known or unknown to the author, and all incidents are pure invention.

Published in 2003 by arrangement with Harlequin Books S.A.

Thorndike Press® Large Print Romance.

The text of this Large Print edition is unabridged.
Other aspects of the book may vary from the original edition.

Set in 16 pt. Plantin.

Printed in the United States on permanent paper.

Library of Congress Cataloging-in-Publication Data

Neggers, Carla.
Shelter Island / Carla Neggers.
p. cm.
ISBN 0-7862-6084-X (lg. print : hc : alk. paper)
1. Large type books. I. Title.
PS3564.E2628S54 2003
813′.54—dc22 2003065078

To Sherryl Woods —
a wonderful writer and friend

National Association for Visually Handicapped
serving the partially seeing

As the Founder/CEO of NAVH, the only national health agency solely devoted to those who, although not totally blind, have an eye disease which could lead to serious visual impairment, I am pleased to recognize Thorndike Press* as one of the leading publishers in the large print field.

Founded in 1954 in San Francisco to prepare large print textbooks for partially seeing children, NAVH became the pioneer and standard setting agency in the preparation of large type.

Today, those publishers who meet our standards carry the prestigious "Seal of Approval" indicating high quality large print. We are delighted that Thorndike Press is one of the publishers whose titles meet these standards. We are also pleased to recognize the significant contribution Thorndike Press is making in this important and growing field.

Lorraine H. Marchi, L.H.D.
Founder/CEO
NAVH

* Thorndike Press encompasses the following imprints: Thorndike, Wheeler, Walker and Large Print Press.

1

"Antonia . . ."

Antonia Winter stopped abruptly in the middle of the mostly empty hospital parking garage, certain she'd heard someone whisper her name. She glanced at the parked cars and the exits, but saw no one else. She took a cautious step forward, her dress shoes echoing on the concrete. She'd changed from the more casual clothes she wore in the E.R. — she had a dinner date in Back Bay.

It was tension, she decided. Simple tension had her turning ordinary garage sounds into someone whispering her name.

"Antonia Winter . . . Dr. Winter . . ."

She gasped and ran the last five steps to her car, clicking the button on her key that automatically unlocked the door. Her hands shaking, she ripped open the door and threw herself in behind the wheel. She hit the button that locked all four doors.

This couldn't be happening to her. She *had* to be imagining it.

This wasn't the first incident.

Wasting no time, Antonia stuck the key into the ignition and started the engine. It was just after seven o'clock on Saturday evening. She'd been on duty a full twelve hours. She was a trauma physician in the busy emergency room of a downtown Boston hospital. None of her cases today had been easy ones. But that was her job, and she was good at it — she was accustomed to dealing with its demands. She wasn't one to go off the deep end and imagine things that hadn't happened, draw the most dramatic conclusion to innocent events.

At least she'd never been that sort. Maybe the demands of the rest of her life had finally gotten to her. Demands like Hank Callahan, she thought. He was her dinner date that night. She'd been half in love with him for months, but their relationship had complications. Her work, his work. Her family. His past. Her past.

Hank . . .

No. She couldn't blame him — she wouldn't.

She wasn't hearing things or making up things that hadn't happened. That was the problem. They were *real.*

Someone had just whispered her name

in the parking garage.

She edged out of her space, glancing in the rearview mirror and side mirror every few yards as she made her way to the exit. She almost asked the parking attendant if he'd heard anything, but she knew he wouldn't have. Once out on the street, she forced herself to take several deep breaths.

Yesterday, it had been an anonymous instant message. The third in a row. *Your patients trust you, Dr. Winter. What if you betrayed their trust?*

All were on the same theme. A doctor's trust. A doctor's betrayal of that trust. Without going into detail, she'd asked a friend more familiar with computers than she was about instant messages, and he'd said that tracking down an instant messenger who wanted to remain anonymous was very difficult, if not impossible.

There was nothing overtly threatening in the messages. And certainly no mention of Hank Callahan, a candidate for an open U.S. Senate seat from the Commonwealth of Massachusetts. The election was the first Tuesday in November, less than two months away. If the messages had mentioned him, Antonia would have to report them, tell Hank. She didn't want to cause an unnecessary stir — she wanted a sensible explanation for what was going on. If something *was* going on. She still didn't want to believe someone was trying to get under her skin. Creep her out.

But who would want to?

Why?

Was someone stalking her?

No. It couldn't be. Tension, fatigue and her imagination must have turned the whir of a car engine or an exhaust fan into someone whispering her name. Maybe the instant messages were from someone whose screen name she just didn't remember. A friend or colleague working on a paper or struggling with an ethical question, idly instant messaging her. Maybe they weren't meant to be anonymous or creepy.

But when she reached the restaurant, Antonia paid extra to have her car valet parked and avoided another parking garage. She stood in the warm evening air and took several deep breaths to calm herself. *There. It'll be all right. I can do this.*

She had on a simple black dress, black stockings, black heels. Gold earrings. Her dark auburn hair, chin-length and straight, was tucked neatly behind her ears. No lipstick — she didn't have time for it now.

As promised, Hank was waiting for her at their table. He was, she thought as she smiled at him and waved, the most drop-dead handsome man she'd ever met. Forty-one and tall, with graying dark hair, a square jaw and eyes so blue they took her breath away. She'd met him last November in Cold Ridge, her small hometown in the White Mountains of New Hampshire. Almost a year ago, she realized. He'd just thrown his hat into the senate campaign in bordering Massachusetts. His weekend in New Hampshire was to have been a break. Hiking with his air force pals, Tyler North and Manny Carrera. Instead they'd come upon Antonia's younger sister, Carine, a nature photographer, being shot at in the woods. Later that same weekend, Hank, Ty and Manny had rescued a wealthy Boston couple stranded on the ridge for which her hometown was named.

Complications, Antonia thought. So many complications.

Hank smiled, getting to his feet. Other diners watched. He was a man in the spotlight. There didn't seem to be any reporters around, but she couldn't know for certain, another reminder that it wasn't just her reputation as a respected physician that would suffer if she rushed to judgment or cried wolf about a possible stalker. His would, too, as a man who was asking Massachusetts voters to trust him. With just weeks left in the campaign, she had to be sure before she said anything, although she had to admit, her own nature made her reluctant to speak up. She was thirty-five and accustomed to handling her own problems.

But it wasn't just Hank's campaign or her own reserve that made her cautious — it was Hank himself. He was a Massachusetts Callahan, the current most visible member of a visible family of dedicated men and women who were expected to do their share in the military, in public service and in business. Hank had left the air force two years ago as a major, a helicopter pilot who'd flown countless search-and-rescue missions: on his last mission, he and a team of pararescuers had performed the dangerous high seas recovery of five fishermen whose boat had capsized. It had put his picture on the front pages of newspapers across the country. While emergency operations conducted in conjunction with civilian agencies sometimes hit the press, his many combat search-and-rescues hadn't received such coverage — Antonia had learned that the military didn't necessarily publicize when and how it went after aircrews downed behind enemy lines.

Hank would come to her rescue in a heartbeat.

And not just because he was trained to rescue people.

He lost his family ten years ago when his wife and young daughter were killed in a car accident while he was serving overseas. It still haunted him — everyone knew it, could see it. He wasn't even on the continent when the accident happened, a head-on collision with a car driving on the wrong side of the interstate. The other driver was a woman in her mid-fifties who'd had a stroke. Brittany Callahan, three, was killed instantly. Her mother, Lisa, thirty, never regained consciousness and died in the hospital three hours later. Hank wasn't with them — it wasn't possible for him to have been with them. But he didn't look at it that way, at least not emotionally, and probably never would, no matter how much he'd come to accept that his wife and daughter were gone.

No, Antonia thought, making her way to their table. She couldn't just *think* she might have a stalker or some weirdo trying to get under her skin. She had to be certain before she breathed a word of her fears to anyone — even Hank. Maybe even especially Hank.

* * *

Robert Prancer peered through the restaurant window. The bitch doctor was sitting across a small, candlelit table, drinking wine and having dinner with the wannabe senator.

Didn't she know?

Robert had to struggle to keep from screaming into the window and drawing attention to himself. Damn it, didn't she *know* what she was doing to him? Seeing her with another man. Knowing she didn't care about him. That all his fantasies were just that. Fantasies. Delusions.

He didn't know what to do. He'd been lashing out, acting on impulse for the past couple of days. But there was no satisfaction in instant messages — he couldn't see her getting them, could only imagine the look on her face. Her curiosity about who it was, whether the messages meant anything. Was she in danger? Was someone trying to scare her? She wouldn't know for sure. He'd designed the messages so she wouldn't.

And she wouldn't overreact. Not Antonia Winter, M.D. Robert had watched her work for almost three years. She wasn't one to panic. Her coolness under stress was just all the more reason to build to a crescendo and see her quivering with fear, incoherent with it, begging for her life.

He thought a moment, watching the two in the restaurant laughing with the waiter. Was that really what he wanted? Dr. Bitch begging for her life? Was he willing to go that far?

Farther?

Tonight in the parking garage — brilliant. He'd heard her stop and gasp. But, still, he couldn't see her.

And he wanted to, he realized. He really, really wanted to.

He'd taken the subway from the hospital. He could still smell oil from where he'd sat on the concrete floor in the parking garage. How had he missed a damn oil slick the size of the Exxon Valdez spill? Fucking thing was huge. But he hadn't dared to move. He'd spotted Antonia Winter, M.D., Dr. Winter, the bitch doctor — he'd spotted her walking to her car, her heels *click-clicking* on the concrete. She was in a rush to see the wannabe senator. She didn't rush with her patients. Then she was all calm and empathetic and dedicated.

What crap.

Robert thought back to a few weeks ago when he had shot himself in the foot and had gotten a good dose of her idea of dedication to her patients. She'd turned him in. He'd had to explain the gun to the cops and the shooting himself in the foot to them and the shrinks. Took him days and days to get *that* all straightened out. His damn foot still hurt. He'd meant only to get her attention, try to bridge the gap between them. Her a doctor, him a fucking floor-mopper in the same hospital. He figured he needed to do something dramatic to test her, as a doctor, as a woman. As *the* woman. He had never loved anyone else. Never. He'd been completely true to her.

He should have shot someone else. Another of the floor-moppers, maybe. Get her attention that way. He could have delivered the victim to her. She liked heroes, right? Look at the hero wannabe senator, saving pilots and fishermen.

Live and learn.

After his foot healed, it was back to pushing his broom and wringing out his mop in the E.R. Putting up with the assholes and losers who thought it was a good job, patronizing doctors and nurses and administrators who told him what a contribution the cleaning crews made. Listening to them all talk about a hard day's work for a hard day's pay and how the hospital couldn't run without it being clean. His co-workers bought lottery tickets and followed the Red Sox and took their kids to school, exchanged recipes and fifty-cents-off coupons and thought they had a life.

Robert had a goddamn 156 IQ. He knew he should be running the place. His nitwit co-workers didn't see that. They teased him about his name. *Dancer and Prancer, Comet and Vixen* . . .

He didn't tell them his zero of a mother had made it up. He'd never known his father. She probably hadn't, either. But leave it to her to name her one and only son after a reindeer. She'd died when he was eleven. Good riddance. Stupid people annoyed him.

He'd thought Antonia Winter had recognized his brilliance, his potential. He'd seen in her a kindred soul. A soul mate. A woman who understood him.

Fat chance.

He walked up the street, trying to control his breathing. No! He couldn't talk like that. Maybe he still did have a chance.

"Maybe."

She was so damn beautiful, with her auburn hair and blue eyes, that straight nose and small, slim body. Brainy-looking but also physical.

His type.

"No." He shook his head, aware of people passing him on the street, looking at him like he was some loser who talked to himself. But he had important issues on his mind. "No, she's not my type."

His type wouldn't have betrayed him.

The bitch doctor had. As a physician, as the woman he loved. On every level. Broke his damn heart. He was smart — he wasn't bad looking. Sandy-haired. Fit. He'd taken up running on her account, before the foot thing.

The balmy late summer temperatures had brought out the crowds. Robert figured the bitch doctor and the wannabe senator would be at dinner for a couple hours, anyway.

Well, what the hell. He knew where she lived.

And he had a key.

2

Hank Callahan had exactly one hour between the lunch at the Cambridge homeless shelter he'd just left and his upcoming three o'clock meeting with local small business owners — enough time, surely, to drag information out of Antonia Winter's little sister.

If not, he'd just have to come back.

Antonia had gone missing on him, and he intended to find out what was going on.

He parked in front of the tenement building off Inman Square where Carine Winter had rented an apartment in late spring, a move that had caught her family and friends by surprise. She didn't belong in Cambridge. She belonged up in Cold Ridge, New Hampshire. She should be taking pictures of birds and mountain scenes, living in her little log cabin in the shadows of the ridge that gave her hometown its name. She was a nature photographer, a good one. But she'd had her life turned upside down in February when her fiancé walked out on her, and she'd made up her mind that she needed to live in the city.

Once a Winter made up her mind, that was usually it.

Tyler North — her ex-fiancé and one of Hank's closest friends — had tried to warn him about the Winter siblings, not that Ty had heeded his own advice. He'd fallen for Carine after some smugglers had shot at her last November, and then he'd asked her to marry him. They'd known each other all their lives, but the prospect of Tyler North and Carine Winter actually marrying had taken everyone by surprise.

No one need to have worried. Ty pulled the plug a week before the wedding. He still insisted it wasn't cold feet — he said he'd come to his senses in the nick of time. He couldn't marry Carine. She'd lost her parents when she was three and wanted to lead a peaceful life, and Tyler North wasn't a peaceful man.

But now Hank had to suffer for his friend's bad behavior, too. It had put Antonia at arm's length from him for months. Only recently had Hank managed to get her not to think about her broken-hearted sister when she looked at him. It didn't matter that Antonia had known Tyler even longer than he had — they'd shared a military career. They'd performed missions together.

"The Winters are thick as thieves," Ty had once tried to explain. "Don't let their bickering fool you. Hurt one, you've hurt them all. They're about as hard-bitten and stubborn as anyone you'll ever meet."

It was true. When it came to being hard-bitten and stubborn, the only one who rivaled the Winter sisters, their brother, Nate, and Gus, the uncle who'd raised them, was Tyler North. He'd grown up in Cold Ridge and still called it home, although he was a master sergeant in the air force, a nearly twenty-year pararescue veteran. Ty had seen it all, and he'd done it all.

Except marry Carine Winter.

Which complicated Hank's life, but he wasn't just going to stop being Ty's friend. The mutual respect they'd developed for each other in the military had solidified into friendship now that Hank was out of the military and fraternization rules were no longer an issue. Ty was the one who'd invited him to Cold Ridge in the first place. Otherwise, Hank thought, he wouldn't have been there last November to meet the Winter sisters.

But he knew he had to be patient.

Although Antonia didn't say so in as many words — she didn't have to — she felt she was being disloyal to her sister by falling for one of Carine's ex-fiancé's military pals.

Hank gritted his teeth. He'd trust Tyler North with his life, but there were days he wouldn't mind tracking his friend down wherever he was — on a training mission, deployed to some remote battlefield — and knocking the shit out of him. Had he *ever* intended to marry Carine?

Five minutes, Hank thought. Five minutes he'd wasted dithering over his situation. He couldn't change reality. Carine Winter was living in Cambridge. She insisted she hated Tyler North. And Antonia was on her sister's side. Unconditionally.

And Hank now had less than fifty-five minutes to get her younger sister to give him the information he wanted.

He kicked open his car door and climbed out onto the busy, narrow street of multifamily houses. He'd been in combat. He'd ditched helicopters. He'd endured the media onslaught that came with being a candidate for the senate. Damn it, he could handle the Winter sisters.

Carine almost didn't let him in.

Hank frowned at her through the grimy front door window. "Carine — I'm worried about Antonia. I just want to talk to you."

It wasn't true — he wanted to pump her for information. But with obvious misgiving, Carine pulled the door open about a foot. She was two inches taller than her sister, her auburn hair a couple of tones darker, but she and Antonia had the same blue eyes. "She's not here."

"I know that. May I come in?"

"I'm kind of busy —"

"Carine. Please."

She sighed, and he could see that her heart wasn't into being rude to him. It wouldn't be nearly as satisfying as pitching Tyler off a cliff, which, last Hank had heard, was what she'd threatened to do the next time she saw him. But Ty hadn't surfaced in Cold Ridge in months, and Carine, too, had stayed away. Hank could see it worried Antonia, but Carine's state of mind was, by unspoken agreement, a forbidden topic.

She opened the door the rest of the way and pretended to peer out onto the street. "What, no entourage?"

"I came alone."

"Really? They let you do that?" She didn't bother to curb her sarcasm, as if she lumped him in with Ty and he deserved for her to give him a hard time was the best she could get. "Do you have a limo waiting? I'll bet your people keep a tight leash on you —"

Hank unclenched his jaw and tried to smile. "I'm just a guy doing his best."

"Yeah, right. That's what all the ex-rescue pilots turned senate candidates say." But her sarcasm let up, her tone lightening slightly as she sighed, then motioned at him. "Okay, okay. You might as well come in."

He followed her down a poorly lit hall to her first-floor apartment. The place was the polar opposite of her little log cabin in New Hampshire, just down the road from the sprawling center-chimney house Tyler North had inherited from his wacky mother.

"I see you've been painting," Hank said, noting the bright colors of all the walls and furnishings in the apartment's adjoining three rooms. He couldn't see the bathroom, but expected it, too, was bright. The kitchen cabinets were a citrus-green, the walls mango-colored.

"My landlord said I could."

"You don't think he meant white?"

She gave him a quick, unexpected smile

and sat at her kitchen table, painted a cheerful lavender-blue. Somehow, all the colors worked together. "I didn't ask."

A photograph of a red-tailed hawk hung above the flea-market table. It gave Hank a start, as most of Carine's photographs did. She had a gift, one she couldn't be using to its fullest in Boston. He'd avoided asking Antonia too many questions about her younger sister, but the last he'd heard, Carine had taken a commercial assignment with a Newbury Street shop.

But he stayed focused on his mission. "I'm wondering if you've talked to Antonia recently."

"Why?"

Hank didn't respond to her reflexive suspicion. "We had dinner together on Saturday." That was three days ago, he thought. Three days and not a word from her. "She'd just come off shift and was tired, maybe a little on edge. She seemed to have a lot on her mind. She said she planned to go out of town for a few days to work on a journal article she'd been putting off. I assume that's where she is?"

Carine was the youngest of the three Winter siblings, orphaned when they were three, five and seven, and she wasn't one to easily give up what she knew — even on a good day. "She didn't tell you?"

He shook his head. "I might not have been clear on the dates, or just missed it when she said where she was going. I left several messages on her cell phone. She hasn't returned my calls."

Carine lifted her blue eyes to him. "Maybe you should take the hint."

"Carine, for God's sake —"

She kicked out her legs and folded her hands on her lap in a gesture of pure unrepentance. "How's the campaign going?"

"Fine. It has nothing to do with why I'm here."

She ignored him. "A retired air force major. A hero. A Massachusetts Callahan. A candidate for the United States Senate. I guess you wouldn't be used to people giving you the brush-off, huh?"

"Antonia wouldn't sneak off if she wanted to get rid of me." He knew he couldn't back down, show even a hint of weakness — otherwise he wouldn't get a thing out of Carine. "She'd tell me. She's a straightforward woman —"

"A clean, quick death instead of a slow one," Carine said, her tone suddenly quiet. "Either way, in the end, it still hurts, and you're still dead."

"I'm not Ty North, Carine."

Her moment of melancholy vanished as quickly as it had appeared. "That's true. If you were, I'd have stink-bombed you out on the porch." She dropped her hands to her sides and sat up straight. "Hank, honestly, I can't help you. I'm sorry."

She wasn't sorry. He saw it now. She was stonewalling him — on purpose. It wasn't just her close-mouthed nature at work, or the tight bond between the two sisters. Carine knew something, and she didn't want to tell him. Or wasn't supposed to tell him. Or both.

"Carine, normally I wouldn't be here." Hank tried to keep his tone reasonable. "I'd wait for Antonia to get back and talk with her then. But she wasn't herself the other night at dinner. She blamed her work, but I'm worried it might be something else."

"You, maybe?"

Ty had warned him that Carine could worm her way right down to a person's last, raw nerve. Hank controlled himself, refusing to react defensively and let her see she was getting to him. "Maybe. I'm serious about her, Carine. If my campaign's made her nervous —"

"That's not what you think," Carine said

confidently. "Am I right?"

"You're right. It's not the campaign."

"On the other hand, maybe whatever's going on with Antonia is her problem, not yours, and what you should do is mind your own business."

Her tone was matter of fact, as if he should have thought of this point on his own. Independent, Hank remembered, was another word Ty had used to describe the Winters, right after hard-bitten and stubborn. Hank figured his only defense was to stay the course — get Carine on his side, get her to trust him. But her emotions were still raw after what Ty had done, and she had good reason not to trust anyone, especially one of her ex-fiancé's friends, so easily again.

"What if it's something she can't or shouldn't handle on her own?" Hank asked, trying to appeal to her common sense. "What if she's in over her head?"

Carine averted her eyes, and Hank knew he had her — she was on the defensive. He wasn't crazy. Something was up with Antonia. But he made sure he didn't let any victory, any smugness, show. Too much was at stake. Every instinct he had said so.

But ten seconds stretched into thirty,

thirty into a minute, and she didn't say a word.

Hank let a hiss of impatience escape. "If you don't want to tell me what's going on, Carine, okay, I can't make you." He paused, debating, then said, "I'll just call Gus."

She didn't like that. Gus Winter had raised them since he'd carted the bodies of his brother and sister-in-law off Cold Ridge thirty years ago, when he was just twenty years old himself and in no position to take on three little kids.

Carine jumped to her feet, her long hair whipping around as she flounced across the small, dingy linoleum floor to the scarred stainless steel sink. "What do you mean, you'll call Gus? Like Antonia and I are twelve years old or something?"

Hank leaned back against the ancient counter cabinets. This was working. He couldn't back off — he had to go for the jugular. "All right. Forget Gus. I'll get Tyler here. He can hang you out your window by your toes until you talk."

She stopped dead, one hand on the sink faucet, color rising high in her cheeks. "Go ahead. See if I care."

"I just want you to understand that I'm serious. Something's going on with

Antonia. I think you know it, or at least sense it, but you want to make this hard because you promised her you'd keep your mouth shut." Hank let his tone soften slightly and attempted a smile. "I figure Antonia will forgive you for talking if you tell her I stooped low enough to threaten to sic Ty North on you."

"Meaning you're bluffing?"

"Meaning I wouldn't underestimate my determination."

She let out an exasperated sigh but said nothing.

"Is Antonia in some kind of trouble, Carine?" Hank asked. "Are you?"

"Not me." Her eyes spit fire at him. "I'm in good shape now that I have all you military types out of my life."

"I'm just a senate candidate these days."

She scowled. "Don't think I'll vote for you."

He grinned at her. "You will, and you know it. You liked me before Ty bailed on you. You have a soft spot for us military types." He took a step toward her. Tyler North was one of the bravest men Hank had ever known — except when it came to Carine Winter. She was without a doubt the one woman Ty would ever love, and the dope had skipped out on her. Hank knew it still hurt. "Give Ty a little time —"

"I'm not giving him anything. He's out of my life. I don't even think about him anymore, unless people like you insist on bringing up his name."

She was such a liar, but Hank decided not to tell her so.

"Anyway," she said, "he's got nothing to do with what's going on with Antonia."

That was his confirmation. He was right. There was something.

Carine turned on the faucet and filled a mason jar with water. Her cheeks were red, but her underlying color was pale, the strain of the last months evident. Despite the bright colors she'd used on the walls and furnishings, the place was still old and rundown, a testament to her hand-to-mouth existence. Hank didn't know if she lived the way she did because of the temporary nature of her life here or because she didn't have any money — or because she was just too tight-fisted to part with it. She could always sell her log cabin in New Hampshire, but Hank knew she hadn't even rented it out.

And she thought of herself as an artistic type, a sensitive soul, not a typical risk-taking Winter. Something about her tended to bring out people's protective urges. But as Hank watched her gulp down her water, he knew he had to keep up the pressure. "Tell me what you know, Carine."

She turned on the tiny television on a shelf above the table. Hank had no idea what she was up to. The TV was tuned to the Weather Channel, which was giving the latest coordinates on Hurricane Hope, a menacing Category 3 storm working its way up the east coast. Its maximum sustained winds were 120 mph, with even higher gusts. No watches or warnings had yet gone up in New England — Hope was expected to turn out to sea before it got that far north.

Carine glanced back at him with a studied nonchalance. "What do you think of naming a hurricane Hope?"

"I hadn't thought about it at all."

"We Winters are mountain types ourselves. We've been in the White Mountains since Madison was president. One of the high peaks is named after him, did you know that? Mount Madison."

"Carine —"

He might not have spoken. "Put me on top of a five-thousand-foot peak in the White Mountains when the weather gets bad, and I'd know what to do." She shifted back to the weather report. “I can’t say I’d know what to do in a hurricane.”

Hank wasn’t following her, but checked his impatience. “Are you worried about Hope?”

“Not for my sake. I’m not as exposed here as you all are on the Cape and the islands. Your family’s on the Cape, right?”

“Brewster. We’ve done lots of storms.” His family owned a popular marina on Cape Cod Bay. He spoke warily, uncertain of the ground he was on now — he didn’t want to miss any signals, veer off in the wrong direction and lose her completely. “People have learned to pay attention to watches and warnings. They heed evacuation orders. They don’t fool around.”

“That’s because they know their coastal storms, and they have access to the warnings, weather reports, evacuation orders. If someone didn’t —” Carine licked her lips, starng up at the small screen. “Let’s say you don’t know storms, plus you’ve got other things on your mind. You’re alone on an isolated island, and Hurricane Hope doesn’t turn out to sea — you could be in a mess real fast, couldn’t you?”

“You could. But that’s theoretical. I don’t know how you could be alone on an island off the Cape —”

"It could happen. Even these days."

Hank narrowed his eyes on her, aware of her intensity of emotion — her ambivalence about what she was doing. "Carine, are you saying Antonia is alone on an island, without access to storm reports and evacuation orders?"

"I'm not saying anything."

But her breathing was more shallow and rapid as she shifted back to him, as if she was waiting for him to figure out what she was saying and do what she already knew he would do.

He fished out his cell phone and dialed Tyler North's cell number. Ty was stationed at Hurlburt Field Air Force Base in the Florida panhandle, where he was assigned to the 16th Special Operations Wing as the Team Leader of a Special Tactics Team. God only knew where he'd be. Hank expected to have to leave a message, but Ty picked up on the second ring. "North."

"Where are you?"

"Florida. Drinking a beer. You?"

"Cambridge. I'm with Carine."

Ty was silent.

"Something's up with Antonia. She must have sworn Carine to secrecy, so I can't get any straight answers."

"Good luck, pal. She's not talking unless she wants to talk."

"She's given me a hint. Apparently Antonia is on an island somewhere off Cape Cod, and Carine's worried she'll be stuck there if Hurricane Hope doesn't turn out to sea — or she'll ride it out, because she doesn't have access to weather reports or doesn't know any better."

Ty grunted. "She'd know better, but she'd ride out the fires of hell if she thought she had to. Both of them would."

"Yeah. Carine did almost marry you."

"We're not going there, Major."

Tyler only called him major nowadays when he wanted to distance himself. Hank had put him on the spot. "She knew I'd call you."

"Carine did?" His tone changed, becoming more serious. "Then you damn well know there's something wrong. I'm the last person Carine would let you turn to for help. Hank? What the hell's going on?"

"That's why I'm here — to find out."

"Carine's okay? She's safe?"

Hank's pulse pounded in his temple. He couldn't figure out what had happened to Ty. One day, Hank was making plans to attend his friend's wedding in Cold Ridge. The next day, the wedding was off, and

Tyler had taken off into the White Mountains with not much more than a jackknife and a pair of crampons.

"She's fine," Hank said. "She's standing here watching the Weather Channel and pretending she doesn't realize I'm talking to you. I'm guessing she thinks you know where Antonia is."

Tyler sighed. He'd known these women all his life — in many ways, they were the only family he'd ever had. "Shelter Island. You're a Cape Codder. You must know it."

Hank was confused. "Of course I know it — it's a tiny barrier island off Chatham. But it's a national wildlife refuge. I thought there weren't any cottages on it anymore, and it's illegal to camp there."

"You wouldn't get Antonia in a tent, anyway," Ty said. "There's one cottage left on the island. Antonia has this friend in Boston — she's like a hundred or something. She has a life-lease to the last cottage on Shelter Island. When she dies, it goes to the birds, literally. Antonia used to go there to study for exams when she was in med school."

She had never mentioned her friend or her cottage, another reminder, Hank thought, of just how much he still had to learn about her.

"You're going down there?" Tyler asked.

"Yes. As soon as possible. I have a feeling there's more going on than just a hurricane that might or might not hit. Antonia was on edge when I saw her last on Saturday."

"Carine knows more?"

"Almost certainly."

"Want me to drag it out of her?"

He'd do it, too, Hank thought. "I'm not having you go AWOL on my account. I'll handle it. If Carine knows anything that would help me help her sister," he added pointedly, for Carine's benefit, "she'd tell me."

Carine didn't respond, still pretending not to be listening.

"The Winters don't think like normal people," Ty said. "How many women do you know who would stay by themselves in the only cottage on a barrier island with a hurricane churning up the coast? If Antonia doesn't think she needs to leave, she's not going to."

"Any advice?"

"Bring her a toe tag. Then the rescue workers can identify her body."

"North, for God's sake —"

"It'll get her attention. She's an E.R. doctor. She knows what happens to people who don't heed safety warnings made in their best interest."

He hung up.

Hank stared a moment at his dead phone. The surprise wasn't that Tyler North had canceled his wedding to Carine Winter at the last minute. The surprise was that it had ever been on in the first place.

He sighed at her. "You were really going to marry him?"

She managed a halfhearted smile. "It seems crazy now, doesn't it? Are you — Hank, Antonia specifically asked me not to tell you —"

"I suspected as much. And yes, I'm going."

"She's very independent. She's not used to —" Carine broke off, then resumed. "She won't like the idea of anyone thinking she might need to be rescued. Me, you. It doesn't matter. It means we think she's in a situation she can't handle on her own."

"It's not a fun place to be. But if you're there, you're there."

Carine nodded, saying nothing.

"Carine, is it just the hurricane?"

"No." Her voice was barely audible, but she cleared her throat and went on in a normal tone. "There's something else. But she wouldn't tell me."

She left it at that, and for the first time, Hank saw the sadness that still clung to her. Usually it was buried under anger and stubbornness — the resolve not to let Tyler North be the ruin of her. But not this time. "Do you know anything?" Hank asked softly. "Do you have any ideas?"

"I think she's scared. That's not like her." She pushed a hand through her hair and seemed to force her mood to shift from its palpable uneasiness. "Are you taking a posse with you or going alone?"

By posse, Hank knew she meant not just the people who surrounded him as a candidate, but his air force buddies, led by pararescuer Tyler North. But he shook his head. "I'm going alone."

She forced a smile. "I guess there are some things you can still do alone."

3

Follow the wannabe senator.

Robert didn't know how he'd manage it without being caught, but he figured with the 156 IQ, he'd find a way.

How had he let the bitch doctor slip through his fingers?

Actually he knew. It was the sister's fault. She'd loaned Dr. Bitch her car so she could sneak out of town.

Carine Winter, the jilted nature photographer. Robert had slipped into her apartment one afternoon a week ago and borrowed the set of keys she had to Antonia's apartment, had them copied and returned them. Then he'd checked out her laptop and read some of her sent e-mails. Pitiful. Really pitiful. Except she had a tough streak — man, he wouldn't want to be the guy who'd given her the boot.

He'd sent the bitch sister one of the instant messages from the laptop. A stroke of genius, he'd thought.

He'd debated fire-bombing Miss Carine's dump of an apartment, but he had to keep his eyes on the prize.

Antonia Winter, M.D.

Scared. Sweating. At his mercy, the way he'd been at her mercy with his foot.

Begging for her life.

It was the image he came back to over and over as he considered his next move. He knew he should probably have a master plan, but he loved the spontaneity — hell, he didn't know what he'd do next, never mind Dr. Bitch Winter.

He honestly didn't know if he'd kill her. He might, he might not.

Probably he would.

He sat cross-legged on Dr. Winter's soft, pretty bed in her Back Bay apartment. It was kind of a girly room. Elegant, expensive, but Robert hadn't expected the framed photographs of flowers — the little sister's work — and the scented candles, the lace-edged sheets. He'd gone through her lingerie drawer. Nice stuff. Silky. But he got to thinking about how she'd treated him in the E.R., how she was so sweet and caring at first, making him think he might have a real chance with her. That he was right about her, and she just needed him to injure himself to give her an excuse to make a move on him, put out the vibes for him to make a move on her.

Then she turned him in to the cops. She said it was the law, that she had to report any suspected gunshot wound. Bullshit! It wasn't like he'd committed a crime. He'd shot *himself* in the foot! Big deal! She could have let it go. It wasn't as if he'd shot someone *else* in the foot.

They'd left him alone for about a half-second in the X-ray room, and he'd pulled out his IV and made a run for it, shot up foot and everything. The cops caught him in the parking lot. Chased him down like he was a runaway dog. If he hadn't had the limp, he'd have made it to safety. He knew the hospital terrain better than the damn cops did.

Yeah, thinking about his little trip to the E.R. had pissed him off.

He'd found scissors and shredded the bitch doctor's underwear. Bras, panties, slips, camisoles. All of it. In pieces.

That'd scare the shit out of her if he didn't catch up with her first and she made it back here. If he decided not to kill her after all.

It was only his second time in her apartment. He resisted overdoing it. Miss Carine, another loser, didn't realize the keys had even been missing, never mind that he'd scared the crap out of her sister using her very own laptop.

Robert grinned to himself. See? That high IQ at work.

His granny, who'd raised him after his loser of a mother croaked from a drug overdose, said he could do anything he put his mind to, he was just that smart. She'd dropped dead of a stroke when he was sixteen. He'd found her facedown in her rice plate. Poor old thing.

But Robert didn't want to think about his grandmother. He stood in the middle of Antonia's soft, thick rug. Somehow he had to pick up Superman Hank's trail again. How hard could it be? Figure out where he was making his appearance and follow him from there — Robert had done it before. As a strategy, it made sense. If the major knew where the bitch doctor was, he'd go to her. If he didn't know, he'd find her.

Robert snatched up her telephone and hit the redial button. See who the good doctor had talked to last. Why not?

"Good afternoon, Winslow residence."

What was this? Robert cleared his throat and adopted his most polite, kiss-ass voice. "Sorry to bother you. Mrs. Winslow, right?"

"Yes."

He loved old people. Who told shit to strangers over the phone anymore? He kept up with the polite voice. "I was wondering if Dr. Winter is there."

"Dr. Winter? No, no." It was a woman's voice, but she sounded like she was a million years old. "She was here several days ago. She's spending a few days at my cottage on Shelter Island. Excuse me, I didn't catch your name?"

"I'm a friend from the hospital. It's okay, Mrs. Winslow, I understand my mistake now. Thanks for your help. Have a good day."

He hung up before the old lady could say anything else.

Shelter Island.

Robert had never heard of it, but he was a goddamn genius. He could find it.

4

Antonia stood on a mound of sand, beach grass and bearberry down a narrow path from her borrowed cottage and, once again, concentrated on trying to relax. A white-crested wave pushed onto shore. The tide was up. The air was warm, decidedly not hot, the wind nearly constant. A lone bird — some kind of raptor, she thought — rode the breeze overhead.

She exhaled, feeling the tension release in her muscles. She was safe. It'd been a good idea to come down here. She'd bought herself a few days to work, think, rest.

"It'll be okay," she said aloud. "It really will."

How could it be otherwise on such an incredibly beautiful day? It was late afternoon, but she'd removed her watch once she'd arrived at the cottage and didn't know the exact time. Still, there was no mistaking that it was September — the sun was setting earlier and earlier. She'd never been out here in winter.

She was alone on a beautiful, peaceful island refuge, exactly, she thought, where she needed to be right now.

Shelter Island was a stopover for migrating birds, and home to shore birds, seabirds, waterfowl. Dozens of different species rested, fed and nested on the small island. Sandpipers, plovers, terns, ducks, gulls, owls, falcons, eagles. Antonia had learned to recognize some of their calls and signs, but she was still a beginner at birdwatching — she didn't have her sister's skill or patience when it came to birds. But she recognized that she was the intruder here, and she did what she could to keep her impact at a minimum.

Only Carine knew where she was. Antonia had sworn her sister to secrecy, probably a bit of unnecessary drama on her part, but it had seemed to make sense at the time. She'd wanted someone to know where to find her in case of emergency, but she didn't want Carine involved in whatever was — or, more likely, wasn't — going on with her possible stalker.

She hadn't given Hank any specifics. The less he knew, the better. He couldn't worry about, act on or say anything about something he didn't know. A few days off on her own — it was all the specifics he needed.

The wind hinted of the tropics, tasted of higher humidity. It was a reminder that Hurricane Hope remained a danger. Antonia's crackly National Weather Service radio indicated a hurricane watch could go up for Cape Cod and the islands by morning — meaning hurricane conditions were *possible* within thirty-six hours. Evacuation orders would no doubt follow for exposed areas like Shelter Island.

Antonia wasn't sure she wanted to leave. The storm still could turn out to sea before it reached New England. It was tempting to take her chances, bet on Hope instead of her stalker.

Three days at her laptop, she thought. Three days going through patient records and thinking, thinking, thinking, and she still didn't have any answers. Who would want to get under her skin? Who would be so sneaky and relentless about it? She wasn't even sure herself that anything was going on, never mind had enough to convince anyone else. Strange instant messages. Whispers in a parking garage. What did that prove? Did she really want the police involved at this point, digging into her life on every level? What could they do? There was *nothing* to go on.

And that didn't even take Hank into consideration.

After dinner on Saturday, they'd almost ended up at her apartment together, but she was aware of how distracted she was, still preoccupied with the whispers she thought she'd heard in the garage. She knew Hank didn't understand. But she'd rationalized to herself that she was doing him a favor by not telling him. Figure out what, if anything, was going on. Then talk to him.

She'd trudged upstairs to her Back Bay apartment and fought back tears as she'd walked into her bedroom.

There, to her immediate disbelief, she found her bedroom curtains billowing in the evening breeze.

She was positive she hadn't left the window open — but there was no sign of a break-in, nothing in her apartment missing, nothing disturbed. Her window was cracked, and she knew she hadn't touched it. She *never* left her windows open when she wasn't home.

She'd grabbed her phone and dialed the 9 for 9-1-1, but stopped. She was on her way out of town. She could add billowing curtains to the instant messages and whispers in the garage and try to figure out who, if anyone, might be obsessed with her. Do her own investigation from the safety and isolation of Shelter Island. Away from her possible stalker. Away from her sister. Away from her work. And, perhaps most of all, away from Hank.

If given half a chance, the media would dig their teeth into her stalker story and not let go.

With any luck, while she was away, whoever was trying to scare her would pull himself together and give up his campaign against her.

But breaking into her apartment — if it was her stalker, it was crossing the line. It couldn't be explained away. It was black and white. A crime.

She referred to her stalker as "he" to herself and believed it was a man, but she supposed it could be a woman.

Or no one.

When she got back to Boston, she'd change her locks.

The wind was at her back as she followed the sandy path back among the pitch pine and juniper to the cottage. She had on a lightweight sweatshirt, shorts and water sandals, her leg muscles getting a good workout in the soft, shifting sand. The cottage was tiny and rustic, classic

Cape Cod with its weathered cedar shingles, white trim and blue-painted doors. It sat on what passed for high ground on Shelter Island, its front porch overlooking Nantucket Sound.

Antonia had met Babs Winslow when she was in medical school and Babs was volunteering at the hospital. Despite their age difference, they became friends. Babs was a true blueblood eccentric. Wealthy, but not one for anything flashy. She hadn't made improvements to her cottage in years — she hadn't even been down here in years — but Antonia liked its simplicity and lack of modern amenities. A small generator provided limited power for the pump, a pint-sized refrigerator and a lightbulb that hung from a beam in the middle of the cottage's single room and was turned on with a string. Two ancient kerosene lamps provided supplemental lighting. There was no hot water — she had to heat water in a lobster pot for dishes and her sponge baths.

At least Babs had gotten rid of the outhouse. Antonia didn't think the cottage would be nearly as romantic without its modest bathroom facilities. Carine wouldn't have minded an outhouse, she thought. Tyler, either.

When she reached her front porch,

Antonia checked to see if the beach towel she'd hung over the rail was dry, then went still.

She'd heard something. Not a bird, she thought. Not the wind, not the ocean.

She didn't breathe, forcing herself not to panic as she concentrated and tried to block out the sounds of the ocean and birds and listen.

Whistling.

Someone was whistling!

"It must be a bird," she said aloud, hearing her own tension.

But there it was again — and no way was it a bird.

She recognized the tune. It was "Heigh Ho," the dwarves' working song from Disney's *Snow White and the Seven Dwarfs.*

Her first impulse was to smile at such a cheerful tune, but then she thought — *no. You don't know who it is.*

She couldn't let herself be lulled into a false sense of security.

She slipped into the cottage, careful not to let the door slam, and automatically, without thinking, grabbed a carving knife from the utensils drawer in the kitchen area. Just in case. Most likely, a passing boat had spotted her brightly colored beach towel hanging on the porch and reported the possibility of an inhabitant, and a local official was checking on her, making sure she knew a hurricane was approaching and she had a way off the island.

Surely a stalker wouldn't announce his presence by whistling a Disney tune.

But she wasn't taking any chances. Taking her knife with her, she darted out the back door, making no noise as she tiptoed quickly down the rickety steps, thinking only that she needed to get to a place where she could see but not be seen.

She ducked behind a sprawling beach rosebush that grew close to the back steps and, mindful of its thorns, crouched down. She held her knife as if it was a surgical instrument, not something she might use to defend herself against attack.

The whistling had stopped.

Maybe it was Gus. If Carine had even hinted about Cape Cod and a hurricane, Antonia obviously unnerved, their uncle would get in his truck and head south, without stopping to consider that she was thirty-five, an experienced physician capable of making her own decisions.

And who's hiding behind a rosebush with a carving knife?

She groaned to herself. Sometimes Gus

did have a point.

It wasn't Carine, that was for sure. Carine couldn't whistle worth a damn.

Heavy footsteps sounded on the front porch on the other side of the cottage. "Antonia? It's me, Hank. Hank Callahan."

As if there were other Hanks in her life. She almost collapsed to her knees in relief. How had he found her? Carine? It had to be, but not voluntarily — Hank must have tripped her up. Charmed her. Used Ty North to throw her off balance. He and Hank were unyielding when they thought they were in the right and someone was trying to thwart them, keep them from getting done what they meant to get done.

What did Hank mean to do?

Belatedly, Antonia realized that her own behavior must have aroused his suspicions. She supposed she hadn't done a good job of concealing how upset she was at dinner, and then she'd taken off without telling him where she was going. Even if he hadn't seen her agitation, Hank would wonder what was going on with her. She'd hoped he'd be too busy to act on it. Then there was Carine — she'd recognized Antonia's jumpiness for what it was and had asked what was wrong. Antonia hadn't told her, which probably only fueled her sister's concern.

And now, for whatever reason, Hank had tracked her down.

He wouldn't regard crouching behind a rosebush with a knife as the ordinary precaution of a woman alone on an island. Innocent. Unsuspicious. If he wasn't already on alert, finding her right now would do it.

She stabbed the knife into the sand and stood up, easing out from behind the bush. Her sleeve caught on a thorny sprig. As she freed herself, she pricked her index finger, drawing blood.

"I'm out back," she called, thinking she sounded reasonably composed. "How on earth did you find me?"

She heard him inside the cottage. He hadn't bothered knocking or waiting for her to let him in, which made her wonder just what Carine had told him. But, Hank wasn't one to stand on ceremony when he set out to do something.

The screen door creaked open, and he walked down the back steps to the small yard that was mostly overgrown with bearberry and beach roses, with a few patches of juniper, foot-tall doomed pine and oak saplings. Lilacs, long out of bloom, grew along one side of the cottage. An invasive, nasty patch of poison ivy swarmed up a stand of pitch pine that marked the yard's far border.

Antonia noticed she'd pushed through a cobweb on her way out from behind the rosebush. She brushed it off her arm and picked it out of her hair. "Hank, what a surprise."

His blue eyes raked over her, and he didn't smile. "You're looking a little pale there, Doc."

"Am I?"

"Did I startle you?"

"A little." It wasn't an outright lie. "I'm supposed to be alone out here. Don't you have campaign appearances?"

"I canceled them."

His tone was difficult to read. Was he angry? Worried? She'd piqued his curiosity — that much she could see. "I haven't heard the latest report on the hurricane. Anything new?"

"It's not looking good." He sounded calmer, his tone less abrupt. The sun hit his eyes, which seemed as blue as the sky and sea. "It's picking up speed. It could hit the Cape after all before it makes its turn east. That would put you in the bull's-eye."

The bull's-eye. She'd hoped being out

here would take her *out* of the bull's-eye, at least her stalker's bull's-eye.

What was the saying? Out of the frying pan, into the fire. Out of the way of a stalker who might not be real, into the path of a hurricane that was very much real.

"I've got plenty of time to evacuate if a watch goes up," she said.

"How did you get out here?"

"Kayak — a new one. I bought it just for this trip. I know I shouldn't kayak alone, but there were enough boats out in the inlet when I paddled over here that I wasn't worried. I had a water taxi bring my supplies."

"Quite the adventure."

She ignored the bite — the hurt — in his tone. She hadn't told him she was coming down here. It was that simple. She shrugged, giving up on any attempt to smile. "It's been fun."

His eyes stayed on her. "Seas could get rough fast for a kayak."

"It's not that far to the mainland, and I'm a pretty good kayaker. I'd wave down help if I needed it."

"Would you?"

He didn't seem to expect her to answer. He stepped down onto the grass, browned from the long summer, and it struck her that he looked taller than she remembered. He had on khakis, a dark polo shirt and running shoes, but there was nothing casual about him. He had that straight spine of a military man and the power demeanor of a U.S. senator, even if he wasn't one yet. He wasn't a man who took a lot of b.s. From anyone. Ever. And he had to know, she thought, that that was exactly what he was getting from her. She was skirting the truth, hedging, dodging, lying. And she didn't much like herself for it, no matter her excuses and rationalizations.

His vivid blue eyes could be so kind and tender — she'd seen them that way. But they weren't that way now. They were calculating, questioning, alert, making her wonder again what all Carine had told him.

"My sister said I was here?"

"Not in as many words. I had to get Ty to fill in the gaps."

Antonia almost choked. "He's not in Cambridge with her —"

"He's in Florida. He says Gus'll kill him the minute he sets foot back in New England."

It was only a slight exaggeration. Antonia sighed. "I don't get it. Gus wanted to kill him for asking Carine to marry him — now he wants to kill him for *not* marrying her."

Hank managed a half smile, without letting up on his intensity. "Don't try to make sense of it."

She waved a hand and picked the last of the cobweb off her arm. "I stopped trying to make sense of anything to do with Tyler North a long time ago. Why were you whistling 'Heigh Ho'?"

"I didn't want to sneak up on a woman alone on an island."

"Good thinking." She resisted an urge to glance back at her knife stabbed into the sand behind the rosebush. "I suppose a bad guy could whistle a cheerful tune to put me off guard —"

"I'm not a bad guy."

His words were so direct, so unexpected, Antonia had to catch her breath. Despite her efforts not to, she thought of the instant messages, the whispers in the garage, the curtains billowing in the breeze. Maybe no one was stalking her. Maybe she was overreacting to a few odd coincidences because of Hank. Because she was falling for a retired air force officer, a national hero, a Massachusetts Callahan, a likely United States senator —

a man who'd lost a wife and a child, who'd lived a lifetime before she'd even met him. Hank Callahan could easily overwhelm the life she'd carefully built for herself day by day, year by year.

And none of that even took into account his longstanding friendship with the man who'd broken her sister's heart.

How could she let herself fall in love with him? It made no sense, and Antonia prided herself on being sensible when it came to matters of her own heart.

Maybe there was no "let" about it. She remembered the moment she'd walked into Carine's cabin last November and saw him standing there, felt the instant attraction, the sparks flying — all of it, every cliché there was.

Hank moved closer to her, until they were almost touching. He'd grown up on Cape Cod and had been around the ocean all his life — yet he'd chosen to become a pilot. A rescue helicopter pilot.

He eyed her again, studying her. She'd always suspected he had a keen ability to read people. He touched a finger to her hair and caught the last of the cobweb. "Tyler said I should bring you a toe tag in case you refuse to leave."

"He thinks he's funny, doesn't he?"

"He was serious. He said if you dug in your heels —"

"Why would he think I'd dig in my heels?"

"I wonder."

She didn't pursue that one. "Well, I don't intend to stay out here if a hurricane watch goes up, never mind a warning."

"But you're tempted, aren't you?" His expression lost all its humor and gentleness. "What's in Boston that would tempt you to ride out a hurricane on a barrier island instead of going back?"

It was a close call, she realized. Crazy, because a barrier island was no place to be during a hurricane. "We're not under a watch yet. I still have time."

As if to disprove her point, a strong gust of wind rolled over the top of the cottage and rattled the windows. "You don't do brinksmanship with a hurricane," he said.

"Hank, I trust myself to make good decisions. You should trust me, too." But Antonia curbed her sudden feeling of defensiveness. "Did Carine tell you I don't know anything about hurricanes?"

"More or less."

"More than less, I'll bet. Look, Hank, I can see you're concerned about me, but don't be. I've been a little preoccupied lately — I just wanted to come down and clear some things off my deck."

"You don't have a phone, do you?"

He wasn't backing off. She could see now that she'd miscalculated when she hadn't told him what she was up to. She shook her head. "No phone. There's no cellular service, either." She smiled suddenly. "I have emergency flares."

"Flares." He smiled back at her, his grim mood easing somewhat. "You're something, Dr. Winter. Most people would stay at an inn to clear their decks, not sit in an old cottage out here all alone."

"I love it out here." But she didn't belabor the point, because if he'd dragged her whereabouts out of Carine, she didn't stand a chance herself if he decided to press her about what all she wasn't telling him. "Did you come alone?"

"Yes, ma'am. All by myself."

His comment struck Antonia as deliberately intimate, and she felt a rush of heat and awareness so fierce she had to turn away. "At least you didn't come by helicopter. You're not getting me up in one of those things."

But he was good with both helicopters and boats — and she was good with neither. In many respects, she had more in common with Tyler North than she did with Hank Callahan. She and Tyler had grown up together in northern New Hampshire, and as a pararescueman, he was a highly skilled paramedic. But he was impossible. If Gus didn't skewer him for what he'd done to Carine, Antonia thought, she might.

But if she wasn't careful herself with the air force type she had in her own life, she'd end up like her younger sister, nursing a broken heart. Maybe there'd been something in the air that night in Carine's cabin, and they'd both been gripped by forces beyond their control, doomed to fall in love with the wrong men.

Antonia gave herself a mental shake. She was getting *way* ahead of herself. She and Hank had been out to dinner together, the theater, a couple of movies, a pathetic baseball game — and they'd landed up in bed once, memorably, a few weeks ago.

But no one was tinkling wedding bells in the background. Hank had lost a family once. Antonia could see it wasn't easy for him to get beyond just having a nice time with a woman, moving to something deeper.

Which was just as well, because "deeper" meant "more complicated," and right now,

Antonia thought, her life was complicated enough. Was that why she'd lied to him, withheld from him? To put him at arm's length?

"I have a boat anchored on the other side of the island." His tone was matter of fact, but he wasn't relaxed. "It's out of the worst of the wind. We can leave in the morning."

The morning. It was, she thought, a very small cottage. One bed, a lumpy couch. Antonia pushed a flood of unbidden images to the back of her mind. "It'll get into the papers," she said. *"Senate candidate Hank Callahan rescues doctor from island ahead of hurricane."*

"Hate being rescued, don't you?"

"I hate having put myself in the position of needing to be rescued. I don't mind that you're here. It's nice you came after me."

But his eyes narrowed on her, his hard gaze lingering on her face until she had to turn away. "You're on edge, Antonia." His tone was soft, but there was no mistaking his intensity. "Why?"

"A Category 3 hurricane bearing down on me, maybe?"

"That's not it," he said with certainty.

She stepped past him, her arm brushing against his arm, adding to her sense of agitation. How could she think? A stalker, a hurricane, Hank Callahan. She glanced back at him as she headed up the steps to the back door, a warm gust of wind rolling over the top of the small cottage. "What would you do if I change my mind and refuse to leave in the morning, even if a watch goes up?"

He mounted the step behind her and smiled. "Do likewise."

"You mean you'd stay?"

He grinned at her, with no warning. "Gives you a little shiver of excitement, doesn't it? You, me, a storm, a one-room cottage —"

"Don't you have staff and security people who'd worry?"

"So? You have people who worry. It hasn't stopped you."

"I'm not going to win this argument, am I? Luckily I don't have to." She returned his grin and faked a half-swoon. "I'm willing to be rescued."

5

Robert set up camp behind the tallest dune on the Nantucket Sound side of Shelter Island. He felt intrepid. He dropped his pack in the sand and tufts of grass — he didn't know his beach vegetation — and crouched down, pulling up his pants leg.

"Shit!"

Ticks. A million of them on his legs and ankles.

The bitch doctor's fault.

He was maybe fifty yards from her cottage, but she had no idea he was there. He was sure of it. He'd arrived about an hour before Superman Hank showed up on the island. Pissed Robert off, totally. He'd known Callahan would find her but thought, given his good fortune with Babs, that he'd get a better jump on him. Maybe work it out so the wannabe senator could find his new girlfriend dead.

Breathing hard, Robert used his fingernails to pick tiny deer ticks off his lower legs. He didn't have tweezers. Dr. Bitch probably had a medical kit in the cottage with her, but she wouldn't help him. She was such a phony.

One of the ticks had a good hold on him. He drew blood digging it out.

These weren't the big wood ticks, he thought — dog ticks some people called them. These were the tiny deer ticks that carried Lyme disease. It could be treated with antibiotics, but damned if he wanted to get it. Some of the little bastards were barely the size of ground pepper. He'd picked them up tramping through the poison ivy and brush, chasing the wannabe senator across the island. Being brighter than most people, Robert knew if he'd stuck to the path, Callahan would nail him. No point in that. A left hook from Mr. Air Force, and he'd be toast.

He had to think. Be proactive. He could put up with a few ticks, take his chances with Lyme disease.

"Keep your eyes on the prize," he said aloud, still panting and wheezing from exertion.

He supposed he could have shot Callahan and been done with him. Robert wasn't surprised the would-be senator had found his way to his bitch's island refuge. It was getting there so fast that bugged the hell out of him. Now he had to scramble, deal with two people instead of one.

He sniffled, digging at another tick. "You're making adjustments, asshole. You're not scrambling."

Right.

The guy, Callahan, was a stud. Robert had followed him once, seen him in the papers and on TV a lot, plus with the bitch doctor. The two of them. What a pair. The handsome hero senate candidate, the beautiful blue-eyed doctor. Robert was nothing to them. Like one of these ticks that had to be removed, squeezed dead and tossed. But not ignored — nobody ignored deer ticks anymore now that they carried Lyme disease.

A light rain that seemed to come out of nowhere washed some of the sand and blood off his legs, but when he moved, more sand stuck. He was covered in it. He felt like one of those little hermit crabs digging its way out of the wet sand at low tide. He didn't know whether it was low tide or high tide now, just that the ocean was out there, rolling, getting scary on the other side of his dune. He wondered if Hurricane Hope was kicking up the surf or if this was normal.

If Hope hit, he'd be swept away out here behind his dune. Drown in the storm surge. Get hit by flying debris.

Callahan's boat was anchored in shallow water on the other side of the island. Robert had come over by water taxi, telling the guy this big lie about meeting a friend and kayaking out before the hurricane had a chance to move in. It hadn't occurred to him until the taxi boat bounced back over the waves that now he was stranded out here, too. The only way off the fucking island was Callahan's boat and the bitch doctor's kayak, which Robert had spotted in the brush. Something to consider in his future planning.

He'd swiped the kayak paddle. That was thinking ahead. Antonia Winter wasn't going anywhere unless Robert wanted her to.

Granny used to tell him that even as smart as he was, she was afraid he didn't think like regular people. He used to think she was just a sweet old stick in the mud with no imagination, no sense of adventure, but nowadays, sometimes, he wondered if she'd been on to something after all. Here he was, stranded, on an island — a goddamn wildlife refuge — a hurricane on the way, deticking himself, risking his life — and for what? *A little payback. A little justice in this world. That's what.*

It made him sick, thinking about himself in pain, with the bloody foot, hoping Antonia — Sweet Antonia, he used to call her — would give him some kind of hint that she was interested in him. He'd fantasized that she'd seize the opportunity he'd provided for her and let down her guard, open up to him, show her feelings. Instead, she'd made him feel like a goddamn loser. A twelve-year-old with a crush. Some jerk-off who didn't have a clue, thinking he had a chance with a woman like her.

After she'd called the cops on him, she'd probably gone out with Hank Callahan.

Robert sank back against the dune, getting more sand on him. Justice. Revenge. She couldn't get away with what she'd done to him. It wasn't right. She'd betrayed him, humiliated him, and she had to suffer. She wasn't the woman he'd thought she was. He'd believed in her, and where had it gotten him? Out here behind a goddamn dune.

Whatever he ended up doing to her, he wanted her to know it was him. No more anonymity. He wanted to hear her beg, see her fear, and know he'd caused it.

"Amen." He opened his eyes against the rain, letting it wash onto his upturned face. "Amen!"

He smelled like salt and sweat and dead fish. He dug his camouflage rain poncho out of his wet pack and wrestled himself into it. It had one of those floppy hoods that wasn't worth a damn. It blew right off his head. He tried tying it on, but the stretchy tie snapped and the end hit him on the finger — it hurt like hell, made him want to kill someone.

It wasn't much of a campsite. No tent. No little stove or firewood. He hadn't even packed a sleeping bag. He'd brought food, but not that much. Some crackers, apples, cheese, all bagged up in plastic. A twelve-pack of water.

He wasn't riding out a hurricane behind a goddamn dune, not with a cottage just up the path. It must have survived dozens of similar storms, decades of crappy weather. If Hurricane Hope chugged north and reached Shelter Island before Robert could take care of business, he'd be in the last structure on this little island. No question about it. He did, after all, have a gun.

A spider crawled up his leg, as if the bitch doctor herself had sent it out to torment him. He yanked it off and tossed it into a puddle forming in the sand behind his dune. He crawled to his feet and looked over the dune, out at the churning water.

He'd never understood the appeal of the beach, the ocean, Cape Cod. It was just sand and water to him. This place was supposed to be a bird refuge, but he hadn't seen that many birds. Maybe they were all clearing out for the hurricane. Maybe they knew it would hit. Never mind the meteorologists and the storm-tracking planes — just follow the birds.

He checked his gun. It was a .38 Smith & Wesson. Basic. But he wondered if he could get by without it. If he played his cards right, Hope would keep Mr. Callahan and Dr. Winter on the island with him, and he could blame their deaths on the storm.

Kill two birds with one stone.

Have his cake and eat it, too.

Robert smiled. "Yeah. I like it."

6

He and Carine were right, Hank thought. Something was up with Antonia. And whatever it was, it wasn't good. He checked out her cottage, similar to countless old-fashioned cottages he'd been in since he was a kid. It was tiny, cozy, with inexpensive furnishings that were functional and at least as old as he was. A lumpy old couch. A heap of musty-smelling quilts, mismatched chairs and dishes, mason jars filled with matchbooks, tacks and rubber bands, soggy decks of cards and the ubiquitous Scrabble game. The bathroom was prosaic, to say the least. He noticed the stack of threadbare towels.

The bed was behind a curtain, the sheets clean and white.

Hank didn't let himself linger gazing at the damn bed.

Antonia said that Babs Winslow was ninety-seven, and when she was gone, this place would be, too. That was the deal. She had a life-lease on the cottage, but the land under it was a National Wildlife Refuge. As, they all believed, it should be.

Shelter Island and nearby Monomoy Island were uniquely located as stopovers for migrating birds, their spits of sand at the elbow of Cape Cod well-suited as home to dozens of species of rare and endangered birds. And time and time again, storms had rearranged what passed for land along this exposed stretch of the Cape — they would again. It wasn't the best spot for the trophy houses that surely would have doomed Babs Winslow's cottage long before now. Development pressures, the skyrocketing prices of beachfront land, were tough to resist.

But he could see why Antonia liked to come here to think, relax. It was about the perfect escape from a busy urban emergency room, not that getting away from work, hiding out to write this journal article she was supposedly writing, explained why she was here now. They certainly didn't explain her mood. She was a dedicated physician and hadn't taken a break in months, but she'd been on the island for several days — why still the drawn look? Why still the edginess that he'd noticed at dinner in Boston?

He motioned to the laptop computer on the rickety table. "How's the article coming?"

"What?"

She seemed to focus on him, then went pale and suddenly swooped in front of him and hit the power button, not bothering to shut the computer down properly. But this way, Hank thought, he couldn't see what was on the screen. Which made him wonder what was on the screen. He doubted she'd have jumped like that if it'd been medical jibberish about some aspect of trauma medicine.

"The article's coming along, but it's slow work." She snatched up a spiral notebook, closing it before Hank could read her scribblings there, too. She shoved it into a backpack on the floor and smiled unconvincingly at him. "I think I brought my laptop more so I could play FreeCell than anything else. Nights here can be pretty lonely."

"Tonight won't be."

Her cheeks turned a healthier pink, but even that didn't last as she grabbed the laptop and it followed the notebook into her backpack. "The battery's about run out."

"Antonia — Antonia, what's wrong?"

"Nothing."

Hank didn't respond this time, hoping to let the silence work for him. He heard birds outside — common seagulls — and the rhythm of the ocean, the whoosh of the wind, and all at once his own life seemed very far away. The pace of the campaign, the constant questions and careful consideration of every word he said, the burning desire to commit himself to doing what he could as a legislator. It wasn't that he could be himself here — he was himself on the campaign trail, too. He saw no point in pretending to be someone he wasn't. But out here, with Antonia, the "doing" part of his life didn't seem to matter so much. He remembered walking the long stretches of Cape Cod beaches as a kid, unaware of the hours ticking by.

But Antonia was obviously caught up in his intrusion into her escape here, into making sure he didn't stumble on whatever it was she was hiding from him. She zipped up her backpack and shoved it under the table, as if she'd marked her territory.

She sat on a chair that looked as if it'd been smuggled out of a sixth-grade classroom from the 1940s and twisted her hands together. "You meant it, didn't you? If I refuse to leave, you'd stay here with me."

"I make it a point to mean most things I say." He shrugged, trying to take any pompous note out of his words. "It's just easier that way. I never was any good at bluffing."

"It's what you leave unsaid — never mind. I'm in a profession where I have to watch my tongue, too. Mean what you say, say what you mean. But you never know what the other person's hearing, do you?"

"Do you have a problem with someone, Antonia?"

But she seemed preoccupied, staring at her hands as if he hadn't spoken, then jumped to her feet and walked out onto the small front porch. Hank didn't follow her. He remained standing in the middle of a thin rug and watched her through the window as she whipped her beach towel off the rail, tossed it over one shoulder and came back inside. "It's raining. I wonder if it's because of the hurricane."

Hank had seen enough fear in his military career to recognize it in someone else, especially someone as unaccustomed to experiencing fear as Antonia was. She was used to being the calm one in the room, the physician who had to concentrate on treating the patient in front of her — who saw fear in others but who couldn't let it affect her. She had a job to do, and her patients counted on her to do it.

Now she was the one who was frightened

and fighting for control. He could feel it, see it in her stiff movements, in the way her dark auburn hair hung in her face and her eyes tried to avoid focusing on him for too long. But he'd had years of training and experience, too, that had taught him to push back his own fears and focus on the job at hand, to stay calm when it was necessary. Then later, when he was alone and safe and the job was done, he could fall apart.

He wondered if that was why Antonia hadn't told him about Shelter Island. She'd held herself together because she knew she had these days here coming up, and she could be alone and safe and let herself fall apart now that the job was done.

Had she screwed up with a patient?

No — she was *afraid.* It wasn't regret he was sensing, or self-doubt, or second-guessing. It was fear.

She nodded curtly at him, her tension palpable. "You'll want to check yourself for ticks. You don't want to get Lyme disease."

"Thanks, Doc. I'm from the Cape. I know about ticks and Lyme disease."

"And mosquitoes. Did you get bit on the way over here? West Nile virus can be a nasty business."

He pointed at her and smiled, trying to break through her tension. "A good role model would be in long pants, not a little pair of shorts. At least you're wearing a long-sleeved sweatshirt."

"I know the symptoms of Lyme disease. And West Nile." She seemed to try to go lofty on him, just to tweak him, but couldn't quite pull it off. "Most people who get bit by a mosquito don't get West Nile, and most people who get West Nile don't get its severest form —"

"I'm not worried about getting bit while I'm here," he said. "By a tick or a mosquito."

She gave him a halfhearted scowl. "Do you know how many times I hear something just like that every day? *I didn't think I'd get hit, bit, knifed, shot* —"

"And you didn't think I'd come after you." He stepped toward her, not in any kind of menacing way, just to be closer to her — to get into her space, maybe, and get her to relax with him. "Did you, Antonia?"

Her eyes lifted to him. "Why did you?"

"Because something's wrong, and I want to help."

She nodded. "Fair enough. Thanks for coming." All at once her tone was formal, even awkward, as if he were a fellow doctor on a consultation. She added, in a near mumble, "It really is good to see you."

Bullshit, he thought. But she seemed to sense he was about to pounce and shot over to the cottage's ancient sink, tossing her beach towel over the back of a chair.

Hank sat on the old couch, watching her, decided he'd give her a chance to dig a deeper hole for herself.

Then he'd pounce.

He wasn't sure of much when it came to the lovely Dr. Winter, but he knew whatever was wrong, it wasn't just him, it wasn't just his friendship with the man who'd pulled the rug out from under her sister. They were a part of why she hadn't confided in him, perhaps, but he doubted they were much more than that. Still, he knew he had to proceed cautiously. Antonia was a woman used to dealing with her problems on her own. He was aware of the baggage he carried. There had been days, many days, when he'd thought he'd break under the weight of it, but he hadn't. And he wouldn't.

He'd been attracted to Antonia the minute he'd met her in Cold Ridge last fall, but Tyler's subsequent behavior toward Carine had put a damper on their own budding romance. When they started seeing each other again a few months ago, he'd never meant to go beyond having a drink and raking Ty over the coals with her — he'd had a family once. A wife, a daughter. He'd loved them with all his soul and didn't think he wanted to make that kind of commitment again. Have fun with Antonia. Enjoy her company. Keep his emotions on the surface. Don't go deep, he'd told himself a thousand times.

But here he was, with her because she was in trouble — because, he thought, he was already in deep with her.

"You've left out a few details of this island vacation of yours, haven't you?" he asked.

"I'm working on a difficult article. I needed solitude."

"Medical journal articles make you jumpy and pale? It's not me, is it?"

She shook her head, rinsing off a plate. "No."

He knew it wasn't but thought it was a way to get her talking. But she didn't go any further, and after a moment, Hank gave up. "Carine thinks you're more like Gus and Nate." Their uncle was an outfitter and guide in the White Mountains, their brother a U.S. Marshal in New York.

"You like the thrill of adventure."

"My life's much more ordinary than Carine thinks it is."

"Everyone's life is more ordinary than Carine thinks."

Antonia wiped her hands on a ragged dish towel. "That's because she only has a theoretical idea of what an ordinary life is, never having lived one herself. She'll survive Tyler North — she *is* surviving him. She was so in love with him, though."

"She'll never admit it. She thinks she was possessed by demons."

"Maybe she was." Antonia walked over to the couch and, without warning, sat on his lap, draping her arms over his shoulders. "She doesn't like you."

"She'll get over it. And she used to like me just fine, before Ty drop-kicked her into oblivion. Gus likes me."

"That's saying something. He doesn't like many flatlanders."

Hank laughed. "I impressed him with my mountain-climbing skills last fall."

"It's that you know how to fly a helicopter — he hates them as much as I do. But a rescue helicopter saved his life in Vietnam. He doesn't talk about it. I think it was a marine helicopter." She let her fingers ease up his neck, into his hair. "Which is the real Hank Callahan? The Pave Hawk pilot or the man who would be senator?"

"Different chapters in the same life."

"I like having you here with me. I feel safer with you here. But if you hadn't figured out where I was, I'd have managed on my own. If I didn't — if I capsized kayaking or fell off the porch — it wouldn't be your fault."

He could feel his eyes darkening, but she kept hers on him and didn't turn away. "Antonia —"

"You're not responsible for what happens to me."

"Guilt isn't always rational."

She nodded. "For years, I thought I bore some responsibility for my parents' deaths. If I'd been better, they might not have gone mountain climbing that day. If I'd asked them not to go — if I'd realized the weather was getting colder and they'd be caught up there —"

"You were five years old."

"I know."

"It's not the same —"

"No, it's not the same. You were an air force pilot doing his duty overseas when your wife and daughter were killed. But there was nothing you could do to save them, and there was nothing I could do at five to save my parents." He could see her swallow. "I'm sorry. I have no right —"

"You have every right."

His mouth found hers, and she smiled into the kiss, pulling him down onto the lumpy, quilt-covered couch. He'd thought of this moment for hours. During the drive from Boston to the Cape, during the short boat ride from the mainland. He'd even imagined the pitterpat of raindrops on the roof. But her urgency took him by surprise. Not, he thought, that he was complaining. She slipped her hands under his shirt and smoothed her palms up his sides, even as their kiss deepened.

"I hoped you'd come," she whispered into his mouth. "Not consciously, but —" He eased his hand up her thigh, over her hip, and she inhaled. "Hank . . ."

He smiled. "We can talk later." Her skin was warm under his hands, but she had on one of those sports bra things that would take a war plan to get into. "Antonia . . . hell . . ."

"Allow me."

She stretched out under him on the couch and lifted off her shirt and the armored sports bra in a couple of swift, efficient moves. Hank caught his breath at the sight of her. "You're the most beautiful —"

"What was it you just said? We can talk later."

A gust of wind rattled the windows and doors. The old cottage creaked and seemed almost to move with the wind, not fighting it. Hank felt the isolation of the place. It was as if he and Antonia were the only two people on the planet. He couldn't even hear the birds over the sounds of the wind and ocean.

He tasted salt on her skin, savored the taste of her, the small moans of pleasure she gave as he took her nipple into his mouth. He didn't rush. It was late afternoon and raining, and they had no other distractions. He pulled her shorts down over her hips and heard her sharp intake of breath when her silky underpants came with them. In a moment, she was naked under him.

She managed to clear her throat. "No — no fair."

But when she touched him, he pulled back, knowing that he'd lose all patience the second he felt her hand on him. "Let's take our time."

She didn't protest, just took a small breath when he slipped one hand between her legs. She was warm, moist, and he doubted either of them would last much longer. When he touched her, there was none of the tentativeness of the first time they'd made love. Her natural reserve fell away, which only emboldened him. He wanted to touch, lick, nibble on every inch of her — and she urged him on, until he couldn't stand it anymore and finally ripped off his own clothes. He had to feel her hand on him. Her mouth. Her tongue. Feel himself inside her.

When he entered her, she stopped breathing. He wondered if he'd hurt her, if he'd thrust too hard, too deep. "I'm okay," she whispered, moving under him. "Don't stop . . . don't stop."

She matched his rhythm, lost herself in it. He could see it, feel it happen. They rolled onto the floor, where they had more room, and she tried to pause, tried to keep herself from coming first — but it didn't work. He felt her quaking under him. She grabbed his hips and pulled him harder into her, again and again. There was nothing he could do. She filled up all his senses, and he exploded with her, crying out with his release.

A long time later, he managed to pull a thick quilt onto the floor and lay with her on it. He kissed her forehead, realized she was still sweating from him. She looked at him, her blue eyes serious, but not, he thought, because of what they'd just done.

Her voice was a hoarse whisper.

"I think I have a stalker."

7

Before she explained, Antonia felt the need to get dressed. She slipped behind the curtain that separated the sleeping alcove from the rest of the cottage and pulled on fresh clothes. Lightweight sweatpants, sweatshirt, athletic socks and sneakers. It was cool in the cottage now that the sun had gone down. She'd never gotten spooked out here by herself — until she'd heard Hank whistling his Disney tune.

She sat on the bed and tried to collect her wits, staring at the pillows and blankets. She'd never spent an entire night with Hank. But he wasn't going anywhere tonight, especially now that she'd told him she might have a stalker.

He'd want to know everything.

Well, she thought, there wasn't all that much to tell.

She rejoined him in the outer room. He was fully dressed and making tea, pouring boiling water from a dented pan into two mismatched mugs. The wind and rain had died down, and Antonia wondered if they were a leading edge of the hurricane or an entirely separate weather system. Hank had the National Weather Service radio on. A static-filled report indicated that Hope had picked up speed but lost a bit of its strength as it hit colder northern waters. It probably would be downgraded to a Category 2 storm by morning, but was still a powerful, dangerous hurricane. A tropical storm watch was up for the Cape and the islands — it would undoubtedly be upgraded to a hurricane watch before morning.

So much for her island refuge, Antonia thought as she sank onto a rickety chair at the table. Hank glanced at her expectantly, and she took in a breath and began. "I've tried hard not to jump to conclusions."

And she told him, as if she were reciting a patient's vital signs to a colleague, about the instant messages, the whispers in the garage, the billowing curtains. Hank didn't interrupt. He just went on making tea.

Finally, she sat back in her chair and sighed. "It's probably just a series of unrelated coincidences."

Hank glanced at her. "Have you ever had strange instant messages?"

"No. I normally don't have instant messages at all. I don't even know how I ended up with that feature on my computer."

He brought her a mug of tea, the tea bag still dangling over the rim. "Have you ever had someone whisper your name in a parking garage?"

She shook her head. "But I could have imagined it —"

"Did whoever it was whisper Antonia or Dr. Winter?"

"*Antonia . . . Antonia Winter . . . Dr. Winter.* At least, that's what I heard." She winced, touching the end of the tea bag with one finger — it was one of her tea bags, not one of the ones left in the cottage. "Or think I heard."

"And the curtains — you don't have a cleaning service?"

"No."

He smiled. "Gus's influence. You Winters are all too damned cheap."

"Frugal," she corrected, "not cheap."

"Hair-splitting."

She laughed in spite of her tension and lifted the tea bag out of the mug, setting it on the folded up paper towel Hank had also brought. "I'm not home often enough to make a big mess. And I don't mind cleaning. It makes me feel as if I've accomplished something."

"Unlike sewing an accident victim back together?"

"It's different."

He sat at the end of the table with his own mug of tea. "Did you clean that morning?"

"No."

"The window didn't open itself, Antonia."

"Carine has a key. She might have done it."

"Did you ask her?"

"No." She sipped some of the tea. It was stronger than she normally would make it. "She'd have worried."

"She worried, anyway."

Antonia felt a pang of guilt. "I know. I wish I'd never involved her."

"But you haven't mentioned any of these events to anyone?" Before she could answer, he added seriously, "Not that I'm your stalker, Antonia, and trying to see if you've said anything —"

"Hank! Of course I know you're not this guy, if there even *is* a guy. Anyone. It never occurred to me you could be the one —" She groaned in amazement at the thought of Hank Callahan hiding in a parking garage, whispering her name. "I didn't tell you what was going on not because I thought you were responsible, but because —"

"You didn't want to worry me. You were trying to protect me." He leaned toward her, his eyes piercing even in the dimming light. "I don't need protecting, not that kind. I don't care if I'm in a tight campaign race for the senate. I don't care if I become a senator. If something's going on with you, I want to know about it. Period."

"It's not that simple."

"It *is* that simple."

Most people, she thought, would back down under that kind of certainty and conviction, but Antonia stood her ground. "What if our positions were reversed, and I had a lot of important commitments at work and didn't need any distractions, if you thought you might hurt my reputation —"

He shook his head. "I'm not buying it. You're just not used to telling people anything. You play it close to the vest, Antonia. It's not just me and my reputation, my guilt over what happened to my family — it's you. The way you are."

She paused. "You're probably right," she admitted finally.

His eyes flashed with sudden humor. "Probably?"

She waved a hand at him. "You cocky

military types. Honestly. Okay, I didn't know what to do. I'm not sure I realized how rattled I was until you got here and I —"

"Ran for your life?"

"Damn close. Maybe I've been in denial, I don't know. I had this time on the island planned — I hoped it'd all go away by the time I got back to Boston. It still might, you know."

"Or it might not." His outward calm deteriorated, and she could see his jaw tighten. "Damn it, Antonia, what if someone attacked you because you didn't go to the police to save me the embarrassment in case you'd imagined the whole thing? Tell me that."

She drank more of her tea, which was still very hot, and looked at him over the rim of her mug. "You're not responsible for the choices I make."

"That's not what I'm saying, and you know it."

"Frankly, I think I've behaved very sensibly." But her bravado didn't last, and she set her mug down. "I've been so immersed in my education and career for years — I never thought —" She broke off, at a loss for the right words. "Carine wears her heart on her sleeve, but I don't."

"I'm not Gus. I'm not your brother. I'm not Carine. God knows I'm not Tyler North. I don't fit into your life that way. I'm not family, I'm not a friend you've known all your life —"

"Tyler's not a friend anymore."

"He is. You all can't help it. First sign of trouble with one of you, and who did I think to call?"

"Big help he was. *Toe tag*."

"He gave me the name of the island." Hank drank more of his tea, then leaned back in his chair, eyeing her with a seriousness she found unnerving. "All right. You know what I'm saying. I won't belabor the point. You have any ideas who this stalker might be?"

"If he's real —"

"He's real."

She fought a shiver of fear, uneasiness. "I brought a disk with recent patient records on it. I get my fair share of difficult cases. Crime victims, crime perpetrators, psychiatric patients — I thought something might jog my memory, make sense to me."

"No luck?"

"Not yet. I don't think whoever it is wants to hurt me. If he did, he's had plenty of opportunities."

Hank shook his head. "Just because he

hasn't hurt you yet doesn't mean he won't. He could be toying with you —"

"The cat with the mouse."

Hank didn't answer, and she got to her feet, feeling the darkness all around her, just the one naked 80-watt bulb penetrating the pitch black. Antonia debated lighting the kerosene lamps. She didn't even know what time it was. Past dinnertime, for sure. She was faintly hungry but knew she couldn't eat.

"I thought coming here would at least help me clarify my options." She didn't look at Hank as she tried to put words to the conflicting thoughts and emotions she'd experienced the past week. "Call hospital security, don't call hospital security. Call the police, don't call the police."

"Tell me, don't tell me."

There was no hurt in his voice — he was under tight control. She didn't flinch, made herself turn and look at him. "That's right."

He was on his feet, and before she knew what was happening, he had her in his arms. He held her shoulders. "Antonia, listen to me. When you look at me, I don't want you to see a senator or an air force officer, or a man who's lost his family and can't bear to be hurt again — I want you to see me. Just me. Do you understand that?"

"I do, Hank, but you're all of those things. You can't separate —"

"What I can't do is let someone I care about put herself in danger because of me. I can't have a woman I'm in love with hold back on me because she's trying to protect me."

She was too stricken to speak.

"I *am* in love with you. I know it's awkward as hell. My timing couldn't be worse with your sister's botched wedding, my campaign, this mess you're in, but —" He stopped, letting his hands slide down her back, his mouth find hers in a kiss that was brief, fierce and impossibly tender, leaving her breathless, even more out of control. When he pulled away, he smacked her on the butt and smiled. "Talk to me next time, okay?"

"I was trying to do the right thing. You know that, don't you?"

"You're a Winter, Antonia. You're a natural risk-taker. Take a risk with me. *Talk* to me."

"I will, but tell me something first, Hank. You say you're in love with me. I don't mind, because I've been in love with you since I saw you in front of Carine's woodstove. But are you fighting it?"

He stared at her a moment, then didn't answer. "What do you have in here for supper?"

"Hank —"

"The only thing I'm fighting is whether I'd rather eat dinner now or make love to you now."

He'd wormed his way under her defenses, until she could only laugh. "First things first. Always."

8

A hurricane watch went up overnight for Cape Cod and the islands. Mandatory and voluntary evacuation orders had been posted for vulnerable areas. Hope remained a Category 2 hurricane and looked as if it would hit the Cape before it made its expected turn east.

No one, Hank thought, would be concerned about the one cottage left on Shelter Island, even if they thought of it. The spits of sand along the elbow of Cape Cod had been rearranging themselves for millennia and would again with this storm. Shelter Island could take an entirely different shape by the time Hope blew over. North Monomoy and South Monomoy Island were formed in the notorious blizzard of 1978, when the single main island split into two islands. Both were part of the Eastern Massachusetts National Wildlife Refuge Complex, eight ecologically diverse refuges that provided habitat, resting and feeding grounds for a wide variety of plants and animals, in addition to birds.

Hank hoisted his backpack onto one shoulder, Antonia's onto the other as they set off across the narrow island. If the powerful winds and surf and torrential rains of Hurricane Hope rearranged these stretches of sand again, at least he and Antonia wouldn't be around while it happened.

They took a twisting path through stunted pitch pine and patches of juniper, low-growing wild blueberry bushes, the ever-present bearberry and beach grasses. It was just spitting rain, but the wind had kicked up, and he could hear the waves pounding the shoreline. Antonia would never have made it across the narrow inlet to the mainland in her kayak. The inlet wasn't as choppy as the Sound, but, as they walked out onto the beach, which was just down from a fertile salt marsh, he noticed the whitecaps. Even with the stiff, steady wind at her back, she'd be lucky to keep herself afloat, never mind on course.

She'd put on jeans, a polo shirt and a windbreaker for their ride back to the mainland and seemed less strained and preoccupied. Hank liked to think it was his presence. She'd finally told someone about her unsettling incidents — he thought their lovemaking might have helped a little, too.

He smiled to himself, but noticed her frown as she paused at the water's edge. "Where's your boat?" she asked.

Hank hadn't even thought about his boat, just assumed it'd be where he left it. But it wasn't. He squinted out at the water, seeing only whitecaps and seagulls against the graying sky. Where the island's myriad of birds were, he didn't know — it was as if they'd all vanished ahead of the hurricane. "It should be right here," he said. "I dropped anchor just off shore."

"Maybe it pulled loose."

"It should have held, even in this weather. Damn it, I grew up in a marina. I know how to secure a boat."

"But you spent all those years in the air force tinkering with helicopters."

"Tinkering?"

"It's not like you were in the Navy or the Coast Guard." But Antonia's halfhearted attempt at humor didn't seem to work even with her, and she abandoned it. "I don't know what to say. Now what? I still have my flares. We can always try to alert a passing boat."

Hank continued to gaze out at the water, not liking this development, then glanced at her. "Where's your kayak?"

"We can't both take it. It's just a one-person kayak —"

"Antonia, I didn't make a mistake. My boat should be here, and it's not." He studied her, her skin quickly going pale again, ghostly, her eyes taking on the strain he'd seen in her yesterday when he'd first arrived. Her muscles were visibly tight, and he guessed she was thinking along the same lines as he was — that his boat wasn't missing by accident. "You know I didn't screw up, don't you?"

"My kayak's over here off the beach."

She hoisted her backpack high onto her shoulder and, with a nod of pure determination, set off across the wet sand, back along a sloping dune. Hank followed her with the two other packs, and she led him into a stand of pitch pine.

"Mind the poison ivy," she said, pointing to a vine of it streaming up one of the pines.

Her kayak was tucked among the trees. It was a sleek red touring kayak, obviously expensive, obviously new. Fat drops of rain splattered on its unscratched finish. Hank noticed rain shining on Antonia's hair, felt it splatting on his shoulder, the top of his head. Except for the occasional lull as the storm moved north, the weather conditions would get worse — far worse —

before they got better.

"The paddle." She almost couldn't get the words out and had to pause to clear her throat. "Hank, the paddle's not here."

"You left it with the boat?"

She nodded.

"When?"

"When I arrived. I haven't been back here."

He turned over the long, narrow kayak, but the paddle wasn't under it. Antonia checked the brush and the surrounding area without success. Hank absorbed what had transpired so far — his boat gone, her kayak paddle gone.

"Maybe the wind blew the paddle away," she said lamely, then sighed, some of her physician's calm and decisiveness restoring itself. "If someone finds your boat adrift, there might be enough time for them to launch a search before the hurricane gets here."

"It won't be that easy to put the pieces together. The boat belongs to friends of mine in Chatham. They said I could borrow it anytime, and I did. They're in Prague right now. It'll take a while for authorities to sort all that out."

Antonia digested his explanation without any evidence of increased anxiety. "Given the conditions, it wouldn't be unreasonable for them to think the boat pulled loose prematurely and no one was in it. I hope that's the case. Better you messed up than —"

"I didn't mess up. Someone scuttled my boat and took your paddle."

She swallowed, nodding. "I know."

"It means we're not alone."

Robert swore viciously. He was in agony. His skin was burning, itching, covered in lumps and bumps and oozing crusts. Now thorns were pricking his arms and back from the rosebush behind the bitch doctor's cottage.

Just what he needed, more shit gnawing on him.

He was covered in bites and red welts. The humidity was building in ahead of the storm, and he couldn't stand it in his poncho — it was like a damn steam bath, and sweating made him itch and burn even more. He couldn't think. He couldn't plan. But he didn't see what choice he had, and he put his poncho back on, just for protection from the thorns and the bugs. He'd given up on the deer ticks. One ankle was damn near black with them. He'd just have to get some antibiotics when he returned to the mainland. Maybe he could get Dr.

Antonia to write him a prescription before he killed her.

Meanwhile, bring on the Lyme disease.

At least he was well-armed against the bitch doctor and the stud boyfriend. It had nearly killed him last night, knowing the two of them were in the cottage. But now he had no illusions whatsoever. He had no doubts. He didn't have to second-guess himself. He'd done the right thing, stalking her, sneaking out here with his Smith & Wesson. Deep down, he knew it would come to killing her. And killing the wannabe senator, too. It was why he'd kept picturing her begging for her life. Because it was the right thing to do. It was necessary.

The bitch doctor would never let him into her orbit.

He was a nonentity to her. He didn't have the nuisance value of even one of the ticks stuck to his leg, sucking his blood, spreading disease. He was just the floor-mopper who showed up for work every day and once, for reasons that she must have thought didn't concern her, had arrived in the E.R. for treatment.

Well, the instant messages, the spooky way he'd whispered to her in the garage and left her bedroom window open, cutting up her underwear — that all had more than deer-tick-level nuisance value. But she didn't know it was him. She didn't even know he'd slashed up her silky underthings. She didn't know he was the one who'd set Superman Callahan's boat adrift, who'd stolen her paddle, who was out here now, plotting his next move.

That was paramount, he thought. She *had* to know it was him. He couldn't just sneak up on her and gun her down. There was no satisfaction in that, no real justice. Damn it, he wanted credit.

"What's this?"

It looked like a knife handle. He pulled on it, and realized it was a five-inch carving knife. A signal from God! The green light!

Here's another weapon, Mr. Prancer. Do what must be done.

Amen!

Robert wiped the blade clean on his wet pants. Another length of thorn-studded rosebush backhanded him in the face and ripped a trail of scratches across his cheek. It was all he could do not to start hacking at the goddamn bush with his new knife.

Patience, he reminded himself. He had to remember what he was here to do — it wasn't getting all pissed off at a rosebush.

Crouching down, he undid the paddle so that it was in two parts. Too easy to end up smacking himself in the head when it was one long paddle, but one of the halves he could maneuver easily. He pictured himself jumping up out of nowhere and whacking Callahan on the side of the head with it — Robert didn't mind if the wannabe senator never knew what hit him.

A paddle, a gun, a knife. Not bad.

It was his own damn fault he was under the rosebush and not in the cottage. He'd decided to follow his two hostages — even if they didn't know it yet, they were his hostages as far as he was concerned. He wanted to see the looks on their faces when they discovered they were stuck on the island for the duration — when they realized they weren't alone.

Keeping them from hearing him wasn't a problem with the wind, the rain, the ocean. It was keeping them from seeing him that almost tripped him up. Not a lot of tall trees to hide behind out here. Once, he'd had to burrow down in the bird shit.

He sank the boat last night just after dark. It wasn't easy, either. He'd had to wade out into the water and beat a hole in the bottom with the anchor. He'd cut his hand. He'd been tempted to shoot the damn thing, but he didn't dare risk alerting his hostages to his presence prematurely. Mr. Military Man would recognize gunfire when he heard it.

And Robert didn't just want to set the boat adrift — for all he knew, it could float back to shore. He wanted it at the bottom of the ocean.

Even when the damn thing filled up with water, it didn't go down fast. He'd sat out there in the dark, mosquitoes chewing on him as he watched the boat float out into the inlet and slowly sink.

By the time he reached his campsite, he was covered with at least a hundred mosquito bites. He wondered if Dr. Antonia would treat him if he broke out in a fever or got West Nile or malaria or something. She *had* to. It would be unethical not to. Illegal, even. She was the one who'd told him she had to report his gunshot wound to the police.

The looks on their faces when they discovered the boat was gone — it had been worth it. They were back in the cottage by the time he'd slipped back across the island, but that was okay. He still had time, and he liked the idea that they had a few minutes to fret, try to put the pieces together, come to terms with the gravity of their situation.

It did suck. He wondered if they had any idea just how much it did, in fact, suck.

The cottage broke some of the wind coming off the Sound, but it was raining again, not a soft, gentle rain, either. Robert was already tired of it, but knew it'd only get worse.

He had to get his final plan together, but he couldn't think with all the distractions of his pain, his itching, his delight in imagining the two of them scared shitless just a few yards away.

The back door creaked open.

Robert sank low, not breathing, as Hank Callahan walked out onto the back steps.

Superman Hank. He didn't look as if he'd been fretting. He looked like some kind of sniper on the lookout. He had an alert, military feel about him that Robert didn't like at all.

Bastard. The arrogant *bastard.*

He should be quivering! Scared out of his mind!

Robert felt his nostrils flare, like he was a pissed off bull in a rodeo or something. "Screw it." He didn't know if he spoke out loud, didn't care. He wasn't taking any more chances with this puke — time to put the major out of commission. "Yeah. Screw it."

Without further angsting, Robert raised one half of the kayak paddle in one hand and the knife in the other and leaped out from the sprawling rosebush, thorns ripping harmlessly across his poncho. He slipped in the wet grass, but didn't fully lose his footing as he lunged for the back steps.

Callahan was looking in the opposite direction. The wind and the ocean were making so much noise, Robert was able to get a split second jump on him.

Flawlessly, in one effective motion, he hit the major in the kidneys with the paddle.

It was like hitting a tree trunk.

Robert was stunned. "Fuck!"

He'd planned to follow up with a knife in the heart, but Superman Callahan didn't even go down on his knees. He absorbed the blow and swung around fast and hard, his entire body poised for the fight. Major Stud knew how to handle himself in battle. That was clear. Robert did not. He was a floor-mopper — he used to get the shit kicked out of him at school. He could feel the old panic welling up in his throat.

He slashed the knife wildly, catching Callahan in the upper arm.

Next thing, the major had the kayak

paddle. Robert had no idea how the bastard had gotten it. He could feel himself breaking out in a sweat under his flapping poncho. Now what?

His gun — damn, it wasn't in his waistband under his poncho. He must have dropped it behind the goddamn rosebush!

He pointed the knife at the major. Stand off. Robert knew if he went after Callahan, he'd get the kayak paddle up the side of his head. On the other hand, if the wannabe senator went after him, he'd get the knife up whatever Robert could reach first.

"You don't want me to kill you now," Robert said, like he had the definite upper hand and didn't realize it was a standoff. "Then the bitch doctor will be at my mercy."

They were both drenched, fighting the wind. Puddles formed at their feet. The grass was so slippery, it made it almost impossible to get any decent traction. If he fell, Robert figured he'd end up stabbing himself. Then he'd bleed to death. The doctor wouldn't help him now that he'd stabbed her stud boyfriend and nailed him in the kidneys. Forget the Hippocratic Oath. Forget the law. She'd let him bleed to death in the sand. Pretend Hope had done the damage.

That would be it for him. The end of the story. There'd be no revenge, no justice, no satisfaction.

"The storm's hitting," Callahan said, ignoring his bleeding arm as he kept a tight, menacing grip on the paddle. "You don't want to be out here. Put down the knife —"

"So you can kill me and tell the police it was self-defense? Hell, no."

The major didn't react. It was amazing. Talk about control. "What's your name?" he asked, all tight-lipped.

"Fuck you."

"Come on. Put down the knife. You haven't hurt anyone yet."

"You."

"Not that much. I'll let it go if you put down the knife and come inside with me. The hurricane —"

"I'm not worried about the hurricane."

But Robert glanced up at the cottage. The bitch doctor was there in the screen door. *So beautiful.* Damn, it wasn't easy to be strong and go through with what he knew he had to do.

He wasn't going to beat Callahan in a fair fight.

That left him two choices, Robert

thought. Surrender, or get the hell out of there.

He wasn't surrendering.

He turned abruptly and ran away from the cottage, leaping through the brush and sand and bird shit, hoping he didn't slip and stab himself in the heart. Another bad ending to the story. No ending at all, accidentally stabbing himself to death.

But he didn't slip, and he hung onto the knife, so at least he could defend himself if Callahan followed him.

He didn't look upon himself as retreating. In a way, he'd accomplished his original mission. Callahan wasn't dead, maybe not even entirely out of commission, but he was hurting. He knew Robert meant business.

They'd both be scared now.

Robert pushed through pine trees and junipers and splashed through ankle-deep puddles, then rolled down his big dune on the other side of his campsite.

Christ Almighty. The ocean was there.

A monstrous wave caught him and knocked him backward on his ass. He choked on saltwater and rain, the wind tearing at his clothes, kicking up sand that ate away his skin. He screamed in agony and frustration, letting it all out, knowing no one could hear him, and scrambled up the dune, back down to his campsite on the other side. He didn't have long before the water would reach it.

The red welts on his hands and forearms were on fire. He thought he'd go out of his mind.

Fuck. They weren't bug bites. He had poison ivy. It bubbled and oozed and burned and itched and swelled. No wonder he hadn't managed to give Callahan a knockdown blow! He was a goddamn mess!

Robert managed to stand upright, but he could see that the sky and the sea and the landscape were all a greenish-gray now, the wind gusting hard enough to lift him off his feet. He could taste the tropics in the air, feel the cloying humidity sucking at him.

And this wasn't even the full brunt of the hurricane.

Jesus.

He had to get back to the rosebush and find his gun. He dug in his pack and checked his ammo. Twelve bullets. That was it. He wished he had a machine gun, but his .38 and a dozen bullets would have to do. He still hoped he wouldn't need to shoot them, not with a perfectly good hurricane on its way.

Snorting, trying not to scratch, or scream again, he made his way back to the cottage and took up position in the scrub pine, never mind the water dripping off the tangle of poison ivy. Why worry about poison ivy now?

The good doctor would be tending the major's wounds.

Robert knew he had to act now, while they were distracted.

He gulped in a breath and dove for the rosebush.

His gun was still there, in the sopping grass. Leave it to the two losers inside not to know he'd left it behind. He cocked it, so that all he had to do was pull the trigger and a bullet would zip out. He knew just enough about guns and shooting to be dangerous, he decided. Not that he'd ever had any instruction in firearms. He figured any idiot could handle a gun, and since he was smarter than most people, he wouldn't have any trouble. He had no patience with learning things, practicing — he liked just to know them.

He retreated back to his position in the pines. He was drenched. Mad with itching. He used his thumbs to get the rain out of his eyes, figured he was spreading poison ivy into his eyes and pretty soon they'd be swollen and itching, too. But he could see okay now and peered at the cottage. It had two windows on this side, a bunch of lilac bushes — he could see the front porch and the back steps from his vantage point. He didn't worry about the one side he couldn't see, because it had no windows.

But if he could see them make a move, they could see him. It wasn't another standoff since he was the only one with a gun.

Presumably, he thought. He wasn't about to stick his head up and get it blown off. Not the best way to find out for sure they were unarmed. But a doctor? A guy running for the senate, out here after the doctor, no idea she was in trouble? Nah. They didn't have a gun.

"I've got you covered." Even to himself, he sounded like a maniacal John Wayne. "You have no way out. Stick your foot out a door or a window, I'll blow it off. Your head? Same thing."

No response. He wondered if they'd heard him. If they were in there, cowering. He could do it, he thought. He could shoot Antonia's foot off. He was a good enough shot — why wouldn't he be? — and he'd waited long enough to see her bleeding and in pain.

"Scared?" He waited, but still no answer.

"Good. I hope you are. I was scared when I came to the bitch doctor for help. How about it, Dr. Winter? Suppose I give you the same treatment you gave me? How'd you like that?"

He remembered her slender hands on him as she'd examined him. Her soft, kind words. He'd trusted her, believed in her. He thought she'd finally open up to him. He assumed she'd recognized him.

But she didn't. She'd asked him his name, as if she'd never seen him before, and even before she turned him in to the cops, he knew he'd misplaced his trust and affection.

He was a nobody to her. A zero.

Then he thought — hell, she and the boyfriend didn't know he had a gun. They didn't know they had to take him seriously.

"In case you doubt me, here's a little taste of your future!"

Robert fired a bullet into the side window, the gun kicking back the way it had when he'd shot himself in the foot. The loud bang startled him. The wind was howling so much, he didn't hear the old glass in the window shatter. But he saw it, and smiled.

He didn't know what he'd do next, but right now, he had the big important doctor and her hero boyfriend under his total control.

9

The wind blew water and bits of leaves and twigs in through the shot-out window above the sink. The bullet had lodged in the bathroom door. It hadn't hit anyone, no thanks, Hank thought, to the son of a bitch outside. Why the hell take a potshot at them? Just to scare them? Why not burst into the cottage and shoot them both, before they realized he had a gun?

Whoever the guy was outside, he had his own agenda, his own way of thinking — but now that they knew he had a gun, Hank realized, they had a chance. Staying low, out of the bastard's line of sight, his arm bleeding from the knife wound, his back aching from the hit with the kayak paddle, he and Antonia had quickly barricaded the front door with an overstuffed chair and the back door with a couple of extra folding chairs. Their handiwork wouldn't stop an intruder with a gun, but it'd give them warning, trip him up so Hank could act. He had a knife of his own now, as well as the kayak paddle and the determination not to be taken by surprise a second time.

But he didn't think Antonia was up to any kind of combat, and he hoped it wouldn't come to going after the man outside — killing him — in front of her.

Despite her obvious fear, she stayed calm and, once they'd secured themselves as best they could inside the cottage, insisted on bandaging his arm. "Fine," Hank said, "provided I can keep an eye out for our friend."

She nodded. "If I were him, I'd hide in the trees along the edge of the side yard. That way I could see both entrances and the windows. Since he shot the window above the sink —"

"It makes sense."

They moved the table down along the wall so that Hank could sit at one end and still have a view of most of the side yard, without exposing himself in the window.

Antonia set an ancient first-aid kit she'd pulled out from under the bed on the table and rummaged in it. He could see her tension, but knew she had the training and experience to focus on what she was doing. "You should have stitches."

Hank grunted. His arm throbbed, but he'd endured worse injuries. "I should have fed the bastard that goddamn knife."

"Ty would have."

"North's trained to feed people knives." Hank smiled, because he knew she'd deliberately made that comment to get him to smile. The doctor easing her patient's mind. "I'm just a mild-mannered helicopter pilot."

"Ah." She found a tube of antibiotic ointment and squeezed a bit onto a supposedly sterile gauze pad — the stuff had to be long past its "use by" date. "That's *just* what I thought when I saw you take the kayak paddle from our friend outside. Mild-mannered helicopter pilot."

"Scared the hell out of you, didn't he?"

"Yes. He has a gun —"

"I know, but first he has to get to us."

She glanced at him. "You're not saying we have the upper hand, are you?"

"I'm saying right now we're okay. First things first, Antonia. We're doing everything we can."

If possible, she was even more pale, but she wasn't one to panic. "Let's see this arm of yours."

She helped him get his shirt off, and he'd been touched when she blanched at his injury — not because she didn't see worse every day, Hank assumed, but because this time it was him. She worked quickly and efficiently. He watched her, noticed that her hands were steady as she swabbed and dabbed and bandaged.

"You won't have to amputate if I don't get stitches, will you?" he asked lightly.

"Only if you get a nasty infection and we can't get to proper help."

"Thanks, Doc. I appreciate a straight answer. You're supposed to say no, you'll be fine."

She managed a smile. "No, you'll be fine."

He moved his arm the wrong way and caused himself a stab of pain. "Now I feel a lot better," he said with good-natured sarcasm. He wasn't worried about his arm. He'd done worse working on boats as a kid. What he worried about was the bastard outside with the gun. He peered through the rain and wind, but saw no sign of their guy. "I can't believe I let that s.o.b. nail me."

Antonia taped a gauze bandage over the ointment-covered wound with a few deft moves. "You're lucky. The cut's not deep, which is a good thing. I'm not set up here for major wounds and fractures."

It didn't look to Hank as if she was set up for three-inch superficial knife wounds, either, but he liked the feel of her fingers on his skin. "I should at least have followed him," he said. "I don't think he had his gun on him when he came after me. I could have kept him from getting it —"

"What if you were wrong and he did have the gun? What if you'd passed out?"

"I wouldn't have passed out."

She added one last piece of tape, then waited, appraising her handiwork, he assumed. "Ty not only could take on this guy outside, but he could bandage your wound. He jumps out of helicopters with a fifty-pound med ruck strapped to him —"

"I know. He jumped out of my helicopter enough times."

She nodded absently, and he could tell her mind wasn't on Tyler North or helicopters, or even Hank's wound now that it was bandaged. She wasn't trying to distract him anymore. She was trying to distract herself. She peeked out the window. "Tell me what he looked like to you," she said quietly.

"You saw him —"

"I didn't get a close look — I was more worried about you. And you're objective. I'm not. Not if it's who I think it is."

Hank didn't push her for more information. "White male in his mid-twenties.

Five-eight. Blond. Clean-shaven. His hair was medium-blond, curly, long enough to put in a ponytail if he wanted to. He was quick — quicker than you'd expect at first glance."

"Physically, you mean?"

"Yes. Mentally, I'd say he's a survivor. He wanted me to think about what would happen if I went after him and didn't succeed — I fell for it. It distracted me long enough for him to clear out."

"If not for the hurricane —"

"I'd have his ass."

Antonia smiled faintly, but was still clearly distracted. She nodded at his bandaged arm. "I can't vouch for the ointment, but the bandage is just about perfect. How's the pain?"

"I hurt more where he smacked me with your kayak paddle."

She didn't smile. "There's not much I can do about that with anything Babs has left behind. Just let me know if you pee blood."

"Sure, Doc, I'll do that." He rolled his eyes, but he couldn't make her smile again. "I can take on bad guys if I have to?"

"I have plenty of bandages."

He winked at her. "That's the spirit."

"Hank —"

"We'll get out of this mess, Antonia." He

got to his feet, avoiding standing near a window, and slipped his shirt back on. It was damp and bloody, but he was running out of dry clothes. "You recognize this guy, don't you?"

She sighed, nodding reluctantly. "It's Robert Prancer."

Hank had never heard her mention the name before. He was sure he'd have remembered if she had. "Is it a guess, or are you positive?"

"I'm positive. The knife —" She lifted her eyes to him. They were doctor-serious. "I should tell you that it was my knife. I grabbed it when I heard you whistling. It made sense at the time."

"You thought I might be this Prancer character."

"I didn't have him in mind as a suspect at the time. He's one of perhaps a dozen names that I jotted down to look into — patients I'd treated in the past few weeks."

"Who is he?"

But he doubted she'd even heard him. "I thought I'd covered my tracks, so that no one could follow me from Boston. I didn't tell anyone where I was going. I even borrowed Carine's car."

"That all makes sense now that I know —"

"But I — I had no idea. I hid behind the rosebush out back. It seems ridiculous now."

"Imagine if it'd been Prancer instead of me," Hank said. "Not so ridiculous after all."

"You're probably right, but when I look at your arm —" She didn't finish the thought. "I didn't want to look silly when I realized it was you whistling, so I stuck the knife in the sand and forgot about it."

Hank shrugged. "Prancer could just have easily got it out of the sink while we were on the other side of the island. Hell, we're lucky we didn't find him hiding under the bed when we got back. He's probably kicking himself for not thinking of it now that he's outside and we're in here."

Her eyes settled on him. "I'm sorry."

He stood to one side of the back door and looked outside, but saw no sign of Prancer. "If he hadn't had the knife and the kayak paddle, he might have used his gun on me instead of the window. Maybe the knife's what saved my life. Antonia — this guy —"

"I treated him for a gunshot wound to his left foot. I had to report him to the police."

Hank nodded. "It's the law."

"I don't think he realized that. It's surprising how many people don't. He wouldn't tell me what happened — the wound was almost certainly self-inflicted. I sent him for X-rays, and he took off from the X-ray room. I don't know how he managed it. He was in a johnny, he was on an IV, he had a bullet wound in his foot — he must have pulled out the IV himself."

Hank pictured the lunatic who'd come after him and could see him pulling out his own IV, running off with a bullet wound in his foot. "How long ago was this?"

"Three weeks? Maybe less. The police caught up with him out in the parking garage. I don't know what made him think he'd get away, not with that injured foot." Antonia groaned, tense, frustrated. And scared, Hank thought. More scared than she wanted to admit, possibly because she knew the guy outside. "He works at the hospital. He's on the cleaning crew. Hank, I have the greatest respect for the people who clean —"

"That's not what this is about, Antonia. It's about some sick ideas he has about you, not any ideas you have about him."

"I understand he's very intelligent, but he can't get along with people. I didn't recognize him at first when I was treating him

— I was focused on what I was doing. Then I played it cool. I wasn't sure what was going on. I didn't want to embarrass him or make his situation worse. It was an awkward moment, to say the least."

"Think he has a crush on you?"

Color rose in her cheeks, which Hank took as a good sign. "It's possible. I'm usually oblivious to that sort of thing."

"Then not only did you betray him by turning him in to the police, you betrayed him by going out with me. And now if he can't have you —"

She shuddered. "I know. That's what I've been thinking. I just wish it didn't have to involve you. You're getting swept up in something that has nothing to do with you."

"If it involves you, it has everything to do with me."

She said nothing.

He grinned at her. "At a loss for words, Dr. Winter?"

"You amaze me," she said. "I have a feeling you always will."

Hank buttoned his shirt, feeling the throb in his upper arm where Prancer had nicked him. It could have been worse. He didn't want to think about what would have happened if Prancer had managed to incapacitate him. If he'd done the sensible thing and shot him on the back steps. "It doesn't help to try to figure this guy out at this point, does it? He's operating according to his own logic. Did you save his life?"

"I cleaned his wound, which probably kept him from getting a nasty infection, but that's unpredictable. Otherwise — no, I can't say I saved his life."

"He came in on his own?"

"He called for an ambulance himself."

"He wanted you to treat him. It could have been a ploy for attention and sympathy."

A strong gust of wind shook the cottage and rattled the windows, and more debris and water blew in through the shot up window. They'd have to do something about it or they'd end up with the whole Sound in on them. The National Weather Service radio was just static now, but Hank thought it was a fair bet the Cape and the islands were under a hurricane warning at this point — Hope was moving fast.

"We should concentrate on getting through this hurricane," Antonia said. "At least Prancer won't have a chance to surprise us again."

Hank grabbed her beach towel and, staying low, stuffed it in the blow-out window above the sink. "Damn straight."

"If we can't get off this island, neither can Robert." Her voice was less strained, and he knew she was focused on what they had to do now — not what she'd done, or should have done, weeks ago. "He's not going to want to stay outside in a hurricane, not when he's the one with the gun."

"Then we have to get to him first."

10

Robert was up to his ankles in water. High tide, torrential rains, storm surge. Fierce wind that never stopped. He didn't know if it was Hope or the leading edge of Hope or what, but he had no intention of staying outside one minute longer than was necessary. Babs Winslow's little cottage awaited him, he thought, wrapping himself in his camouflage-style poncho. He'd also managed to grab a bright blue tarp that'd blown off the cottage porch and wrapped up in it, too.

He felt like he was in a body bag, but a part of him also savored his misery. His suffering would make killing the two in the cottage that much more satisfying.

Killing someone should have its costs. Granny had told him that the best things came with sacrifice and commitment, even suffering.

The rain and humidity were intolerable. He was clammy, sweating inside the poncho and tarp. He might as well have been breathing water. He coughed, tasting salt, and looked around for any dry ground where he could think straight and put together his plan of attack.

"Robert! Robert Prancer!"

He went still, crouching down low under the tree. It was Antonia Winter, calling his name as if in a dream. He stopped breathing and listened over the sounds of the rain and wind. She knew him now. She realized he was the one out here with the gun. The one who'd attacked her stud boyfriend.

Yes, Robert thought, he was in her thoughts now. He wasn't just some mindless, nameless attacker on the loose. He was Robert Prancer. She could picture him, even if it was with his goddamn mop.

Perfect.

He couldn't see her through the blinding rain. Was she calling him from the back door? A window? He doubted she was at the front door, not with the porch in the way — he'd never hear her over the howling wind, the crashing surf, the lashing rain. What a mess.

"Robert, you can't stay out there."

Although she had to yell to be heard over the oncoming hurricane, she managed to sound concerned, reasonable. But she was an E.R. doctor. She was good at faking concern and reason.

He didn't answer her. The hell with her. This wasn't a dream. This was a ploy on her part. She was trying to play to his weakness for her.

"Hurricane Hope is hitting us," she continued. "It'll only get worse. Robert, you'll be killed if you don't take cover."

"What do you care?" he yelled, despite his resolve to keep his mouth shut.

He knew he was giving away his position. Didn't matter. She and Callahan weren't going to do anything. He was the one out in the goddamn hurricane, and he was the one with the gun. They weren't going to seize the lead from him. What happened next was *his* choice.

"I'm a doctor, but I'm also your colleague at the hospital. I know how hard you work —"

"Fuck you! You don't know anything about me! You'll celebrate if I'm dead!"

He sounded like a head case. He winced, pulling the tarp more tightly around him, the rain pelting on it, bouncing off. He had to *think*. If he stormed the cottage — gun or no gun — they'd see him coming and set up a defense. Ambush him some way. He needed to create a distraction, then move in when they weren't looking. A Molotov cocktail. Homemade napalm.

Something like that. Firebomb the cottage. His hostages would have to deal with the fire, and he could move in with the gun.

He'd just have to be careful not to burn down the place. Talk about cutting off your nose to spite your face.

Where could he get the fixings for a Molotov cocktail? A bottle. Some gasoline. Dry fabric for a wick.

But the bitch doctor hadn't given up. "Robert, please. Let's talk before we get in any deeper. I know you're here because of me." He thought he could hear her hesitation. Her regret. "Because of a mistake I made. Come inside. We'll ride out the hurricane together."

Was she serious? Had his actions helped her to see the light? Robert edged out of his cover of pines, the blue tarp trailing after him like a bridal train or a king's robe. The poncho hood wouldn't stay on his head. He was soaked, rain pouring down his face and neck, and the poison ivy and bug bites were driving him insane. He could feel his .38 tucked in his waistband and realized he didn't much like toting a gun.

Visibility sucked with all the rain and wind. Dr. Winter and Superman Callahan couldn't possibly see him.

"If I come in," Robert yelled, "you and Callahan are my hostages!"

"We are, anyway. Robert, you can't stay out there. You can't!"

That last sounded like she was desperate to save him. Like she didn't want his death on her conscience.

Did she care, now that she knew it was him out here, drowning, in danger of being swept into the ocean? Maybe Callahan didn't look so good to her, now that Robert had taken him on, drawn a little of his blood.

But he fought back any sympathy for her. Who did she think she was, inviting him to join her inside? Offering up herself and her boyfriend as hostages? Like she had the upper hand. *He* had the fucking upper hand.

He paused, fighting the poncho and the tarp so he could get to his gun, get it and his hand out in the open where he could start shooting. Did she really think he was so stupid he wouldn't use the advantage he had? Stay out here when he could shoot them both dead and make himself a nice cup of tea and ride out the hurricane in the cottage?

He could kill her and Superman Callahan without reloading. Just do it. Get it over with.

No more fooling around.

Robert had no intention of waiting out a hurricane with two hostages who'd be looking for any advantage, any opening to slit his throat. No way. Forget letting the storm kill them. Forget prolonging the pleasure of their misery. They had to die now. *He* had to do it.

Then he'd have the cottage to himself. After Hope, he'd find a way out of there before anyone found the two bodies he left behind.

He used the lack of visibility to his advantage and headed toward the cottage, gun drawn, ready to fire.

The wind grabbed the front door and almost ripped it off its hinges, but Hank was prepared and managed to latch it before it gave him away. He stayed low, out of Robert Prancer's line of fire. He seemed to be in the line of trees off to the side of the cottage. A good position, one that he could hold indefinitely if not for the oncoming hurricane.

Inside the cottage, Antonia knew what to do. Hank didn't like it, but they'd agreed that Prancer would go on the attack — he wouldn't remain outside in the hurricane. He'd risk everything, and he'd kill them this time. His little cat-and-mouse game was over. All he needed was the right opening.

Hank had the half a kayak paddle he'd appropriated in one hand and a kitchen knife, not as good as the one Prancer still had, in the other. If he got close enough to Prancer, it'd be a fight, at least.

He heard a shot out back.

It didn't startle him or concern him, because he was confident Antonia had done her part and poked open the back door with a broom handle. Prancer, as they'd predicted, had responded to the provocation by firing, instead of waiting until he saw an actual person. If nothing else, it meant he wasn't worried about running out of ammunition.

As backup, Antonia also had a pan of water boiling on the tiny cottage stove. If Hank failed in doing his part and Prancer got into the cottage, she'd throw it on him. She was a doctor. She'd know how and where she could do the most damage, should she be required to act in self-defense. But she wouldn't unless she had no other choice. She treated the results of violence. She didn't cause violencc.

Pushing aside his misgivings, Hank focused on the task at hand, letting his years of training and combat missions kick in, take over. He stepped into the swirling water and sand at the bottom of the porch steps. Rain lashed at him, and the roar of the ocean and wind surrounded him — he meant to use all of it to his advantage. The noise, the lack of visibility, the sense of urgency. Robert Prancer couldn't be in a good place right now, mentally or physically.

Hank edged around to the back of the cottage, using the lilacs and the weather for concealment.

"Antonia! Bitch doctor!" Prancer had definitely moved down from the trees toward the cottage, but Hank couldn't see him. "Come outside. I want my gun at your head. I want the wannabe senator to see you cower and hear you beg for your life."

Hank gritted his teeth and kept a tight hold on the kayak paddle and the knife.

"I'm afraid," Antonia said. "Not of you — of the storm."

That's it, keep him talking. Hank peered through the dripping lilac leaves and the gray rain and spotted a bright blue tarp about five yards behind the cottage. It moved, and he realized it was Prancer, the tarp half off him, more hindrance than help.

"Come out where I can see you," he screamed. "Now. I have lots of bullets. You can't win."

"All right —"

"Wait." The blue tarp stopped moving. "Where's Callahan? Your stud ex-major. Have him talk to me."

Antonia ignored him. "Robert, I'm coming out —"

"I said wait! Shit. He's not in there, is he? You fucking bitch."

He dropped the tarp, kicked his way out of it as he ran toward the cottage, splashing through the water-soaked grass and sand. Hank could clearly make out the gun in Prancer's right hand.

Moving fast, Hank jumped out from the lilacs. Prancer spotted him and fired — but not at Hank. At the back door.

Antonia was supposed to be inside with her pan of boiling water.

Hank dove for Prancer, hitting him in the solar plexus with the paddle. Prancer staggered backward, and Hank followed up with another hit, dislodging the gun. But the s.o.b. was still on his feet. And he had his knife.

Antonia swooped down from the back steps and, without the slightest hesitation, stomped on Prancer's left foot — the same one she'd treated a few weeks ago. He screamed out in agony, dropping the knife as he fell onto his hands and knees.

Hank grabbed the gun out of a puddle and pointed it at Prancer. "Up on your feet. Hands in the air where I can see them."

His hands went up, but he sneered as he got to his feet. He was white-faced but seemed oblivious to any pain he was in. "You won't kill me. It'd do in your chances to be elected."

Hank paid no attention to him. "Antonia?"

"I'm okay. He didn't hurt me."

She was lying. There was blood on her upper right arm. Hank could see it out of the corner of his eye. "Can you make it back inside on your own?"

"Of course."

He almost smiled. His lovely Dr. Winter was nothing if not independent. "We'll need something to use to tie him up."

"Gus says duct tape works best."

Leave it to Gus to explain such things to his doctor niece. Hank waited until she was back in the cottage, then compelled Prancer inside at gunpoint. He'd lost some of his cockiness, moaning in pain, limping. His shirt was torn, his skin ravaged, his long hair matted down from rain. Blood trickled down one side of his mouth — he'd probably bit his lip. Hank knew he hadn't hit him hard enough to cause internal bleeding. He hadn't got good footing in the wet grass.

Hank ordered him to sit on a chair at the kitchen table.

"Go to hell," Prancer said.

But he sat down, and Antonia rummaged around under the sink and produced the roll of duct tape. Hank saw the blood on her arm but didn't say anything until they finished tying up their prisoner. She had a surgical approach to the duct tape, and he saw her examining Prancer for injuries. She would treat the patient in front of her, even if it was someone who had just tried to kill her.

Finally, she sank shakily onto a chair at the end of the table. "A bullet grazed my arm. I think —" She made a face, obviously not relishing what she had to say. "I might need your help patching it up."

Hank smiled at her. "Don't pass out, Doc. You'll need to tell me what to do."

11

Hank didn't need as much help treating her wound as Antonia had anticipated. He'd flown scores of search-and-rescue missions in his military career and knew medical basics, never mind that he was a pilot, not a pararescueman like Tyler North. But none of them could prescribe medications, she thought, feeling a little woozy and defensive — she was a doctor, so she could write prescriptions. She wished she had something for the pain.

The bullet hadn't lodged, but it was a nastier gash than what Prancer had done to Hank with the knife.

"Why were you in the doorway?"

"I wasn't. The bullet — I don't know how it hit me."

"The police can figure it out."

The police. It had come to that, after all.

Robert, tied securely to his chair with duct tape, looked on silently. He was wide-eyed, fuming, soaked and in pain himself, although there wasn't a lot Antonia could do for him. She sat on the couch and focused on what Hank was doing as he cleaned and bandaged her wound.

"You're going to watch?" he asked.

"Of course."

He worked quickly, efficiently, no visible tremble to his hands. She admired his ability to concentrate. "You need stitches," he pronounced, applying the last bit of the ancient first-aid tape to hold her bandage in place.

It was true. The bullet had torn a gash in her upper arm, but at least it had gone right out again — she hadn't relished the idea of walking Hank through digging a bullet out of her. But her wound did need stitches, if not surgery. She sighed. "I don't think we'll be off the island in time. But it'll be okay. You've done a nice job."

He looked troubled. "Antonia —"

"There's nothing more we can do. How's our prisoner?"

There was a lull in the weather, but the storm was still approach- ing, relentlessly, from the south. Antonia had no idea how long before it arrived. But Robert Prancer was no longer a threat. He was obviously in some discomfort from his bites and poison ivy and the kayak paddle to the solar plexus. His foot was bruised but Antonia hadn't done any serious damage — she'd checked.

Her arm bandaged and throbbing, she applied ointment to his bites and offered him Benadryl, but he refused. She wasn't surprised. As they'd tied him up, he'd spat out his lengthy list of grievances. He was convinced she'd betrayed him as a patient, as a co-worker at the hospital, as a man who had fallen in love with her from afar. He'd adored her, fantasized about her — or at least an idealized version of her. Supposedly not remembering his name, telling the police about his gunshot wound, taking up with Hank Callahan. It was one betrayal after another. Antonia was responsible for everything he'd done since that day she'd treated him in the E.R.

Hank discouraged her from trying to talk to him. At this point, Robert Prancer was a problem for the authorities.

But first, she thought, they all had to deal with Hurricane Hope.

Babs Winslow's cottage had endured countless storms, but there were no guarantees it would survive this one. Antonia and Hank collected towels to tuck under the doors and windows in case water started seeping in, and they filled every jug, pitcher and bowl available with fresh water. She tried not to envision the roof blowing off, the cottage splintering with them inside.

"You betrayed me." Robert's voice was calm, almost matter of fact. "You're a traitor to your profession. Bitch doctor. That's what everyone's going to call you. I'll say it loud and clear at my trial. I won't be convicted. You know that, don't you?"

Hank picked up the roll of duct tape. "One more word, and you're getting gagged."

"Fuck you. Fuck the bitch doctor."

That was all Hank needed. He ripped off a six-inch length of duct tape, but Prancer promised to keep quiet. Hank winked at Antonia. "He'll be convicted." But he went still, then grinned suddenly. "I hear a helicopter."

"What? I don't hear anything." But she stopped, because now she heard it, a steady whir that she'd thought was the wind or the surf. "Do you think — I should get my flares."

But she didn't need them. When they ran out onto the front porch, the helicopter was already low over the island. Hank grinned. "Feels weird to be on this end of a rescue."

"Carine. She must have sounded the alarm."

"Tyler, too. He'd raise hell."

"He's in Florida —"

"Not if he found a way up here." Hank opened the front door and shouted back to Prancer. "I'm looking forward to introducing you to my friend Master Sergeant Tyler North."

Antonia felt a tightness in her chest. Her arm ached, but she didn't mind that so much. "Hank, I've put you in a terrible position."

"I put myself here. You didn't. I did what I had to do. No regrets. No second-guessing." He slung an arm over her shoulder, careful to avoid her injury. "Well, Doc, looks as if you're going to have to ride in a helicopter after all."

She managed a laugh. "For once, I don't mind. It beats staying out here in a hurricane." But that was bravado — she didn't like helicopters. "The police aren't going to like it that a senate candidate was knifed."

"Hell, I don't like it. They won't like having an E.R. doctor shot, either."

The helicopter landed on a relatively dry spot near the cottage, and within minutes, Hank was proved right. Compact, green-eyed, tawny-haired Tyler North, a lion of a man, jumped out. He had somehow wormed his way onto the rescue flight.

Now he was their link between disaster and the helicopter.

Hank swore under his breath. "Damn. I'm never going to hear the end of this, am I?"

Tyler grinned at him. "Never. Dr. Winter? You need a litter?"

"I can walk."

But, actually, she couldn't. He saw that before she did. So did Hank. They strapped her into a litter and got her on board the helicopter, another crewman waiting with Robert Prancer. Then they got him on board.

Mercifully, Antonia, who didn't like helicopters, passed out for the short ride back to the mainland.

Tyler disappeared before Hope hit.

"Marry Antonia, will you?" he told Hank. "It'll take Gus's mind off killing me."

"Carine —"

"She'll be fine. She won't want to get in the way of her sister's happiness. Trust her."

"Is she here?"

"She's here. Gus, too."

Hank had known his friend wouldn't stick around. He knew, too, that Ty hadn't found his way to Cape Cod to earn Hank's undying gratitude — he'd done it because that was what he did, because it was Antonia, and it was Carine. Ty was gone before she made her way to Antonia. Gus was at her side, fifty years old, rangy, totally pissed off.

Antonia ignored all of them and got access to a proper medical bag so she could sew up her own arm, informing everyone who tried to dissuade her that she did this sort of thing for a living.

Stubborn. Hard-bitten. Independent. Hank grinned. For all his faults, Tyler North did know the Winter family of Cold Ridge, New Hampshire.

There were police to talk to. Antonia muttered something about pulling another faint to get out of it, but she handled all the questions with a calm and directness Hank had come to expect of her, and knew he would always admire.

Carine, it turned out, had let herself into her sister's apartment in Boston and found shredded lingerie hanging out of Antonia's dresser drawer, and that was it. She called the police. The evidence led them to Robert Prancer. They got a warrant to search his apartment and found it wall-papered with pictures of Antonia. There were some of Hank, too. Most were smeared with red paint.

A missing E.R. doctor. A missing senate candidate.

"That's when the shit really hit the fan," Carine said with a faltering smile as they finally gathered in a local tavern to ride out the storm. It was too late to make it over the bridge to Boston, or farther inland to higher ground.

"Gus was already on his way?" Antonia asked.

"He was already *there*. Ty called him. The bastard."

Hank suspected no one had told her that Ty had participated in the rescue — the media hadn't got hold of that one.

Gus shifted in his chair. He was drinking hot chocolate — no alcohol, he said, until the storm was over. No one else paid any attention. He glowered at the older of his two nieces. "You should have come to the mountains. What do you know about the ocean? We could have pitched this Prancer asshole right off a cliff."

She smiled. "I love you, Gus. And Hank and I handled him."

"Yeah. You and Hank."

Carine raised her pink drink — a cosmopolitan. "I think you and Hank make a great couple. An E.R. doctor and a U.S. senator. Has a nice ring to it, doesn't it?" She sipped some of her drink, of which she'd already had too much "To an autumn wedding for a Winter!"

"Carine!" Antonia blanched, sinking low in her chair. She'd popped a pill — pain medication, Hank suspected — and was avoiding alcohol. "We've all had too much excitement, I think."

The wind howled and whistled outside, but the inn they'd picked had been around since the late eighteenth century. It was filled with various rescue and work crews ready to go out after the storm had passed, and they all were making no pretenses about listening in.

Carine was unapologetic. "Oh, come on, Antonia. No time to be repressed. Hank's so in love with you. What's the word I'm looking for, Gus? Besotted?"

"Sloshed," her uncle said. "Time to keep your mouth shut, Carine."

Hank, sitting next to Antonia, leaned in close to her. "Your sister's right. I am in love with you. Besotted."

"I'm feeling light-headed." Antonia sipped her water. "I think it must be the medication. I forget what I took —"

"You didn't forget," Hank said.

She smiled. "No, I didn't." She couldn't seem to stop herself from giggling, something Hank doubted Antonia Winter, M.D., did often enough. "Oh, God. I love you so much. I have from the second I laid eyes on you. You remember? You were standing in front of the woodstove in Carine's cabin."

"I remember. I knew you were stricken." He grinned at her. "I could tell."

Carine sniffled. "I love happy endings."

The two auburn-haired, blue-eyed sisters started giggling, and Gus rolled his eyes and motioned to the bartender. "No more of those pink drinks." He looked darkly over at Hank. "You set the date, you're sticking to it. You got that? I'm not mending another broken heart."

Hank nodded but said nothing. Antonia touched his thigh under the table. "We'll make it a simple wedding."

"Not account of me, you won't," Carine said, shaking her head adamantly. "Hank, if you want Tyler to be in your wedding —"

"Carine!" Antonia sat up straight, more alert now. "We wouldn't do that to you! You're going to be my maid of honor."

"Do what to me?" She set her jaw in that stubborn Winter way that Hank had come to know. “I’ve known Ty since we were tots. I have the scars to prove it. It’s no big deal. He can be in your wedding.”

“He’ll be out of the country,” Hank said quietly.

Carine scoffed. “What, on a secret mission?”

“Maybe.”

But someone at the bar pointed to the television, and a meteorologist was saying what they could all feel — hurricane force winds were hitting Cape Cod.

Hope weakened rapidly and didn’t do its worst to Cape Cod. Damage would be limited mostly to flooding, torn shingles, trees down, flying debris, lost boats. Everyone in the tavern agreed they were lucky. They’d dodged disaster.

A Coast Guard helicopter flew over Shelter Island after Hope had moved on out to sea, and the pilot reported that Babs Winslow’s cottage had survived with just a few shingles torn off and a window blown out.

Antonia felt a pain in her gut, remembering that Robert Prancer had shot out the window. The damage wasn’t from Hope.

Her quiet refuge was now a crime scene.

The rescue and work crews had dispersed, but she and her sister and uncle — and Hank — remained in the tavern. The bartender passed out free sandwiches and reported media swarming in the lobby.

Gus grinned. "Must be because of me."

Carine, who'd fallen asleep on their uncle's shoulder as if she were a little girl again, elbowed him in the stomach. "Gus, you're not that funny."

Antonia realized they were just trying to distract her. They'd rehashed the events on the island all through the storm, tried to make sense of Robert Prancer and his motives, his reasoning, but he clearly operated according to his own logic, reacting to events according to whatever he was feeling at the time. He'd never had a clear, specific, calculated plan, which, in a way, made him even more frightening. There was no way to predict what he'd do. Taunt her. Scare her. Hurt her. Kill her.

But she and Gus and Carine, and Nate, were a family who'd seen their share of crises, and they knew how to deal with them.

Hank tucked stray locks of her hair behind her ear. "Looks like I need to conduct an impromptu press conference."

She nodded. "They'll want to know everything."

"I plan to tell them everything. I'm a man who was worried about the woman I love, and I went to her." He kissed her on the forehead. "Do you want to be there?"

"At your side?" She smiled, kissing him softly. "Always."

The employees of Thorndike Press hope you have enjoyed this Large Print book. All our Thorndike and Wheeler Large Print titles are designed for easy reading, and all our books are made to last. Other Thorndike Press Large Print books are available at your library, through selected bookstores, or directly from us.

For information about titles, please call:

(800) 223-1244

or visit our Web site at:

www.gale.com/thorndike
www.gale.com/wheeler

To share your comments, please write:

Publisher
Thorndike Press
295 Kennedy Memorial Drive
Waterville, ME 04901